# THE BRAIN SUCKER

# THE BRAIN SUCKER

## GLENN WOOD

WALKER
BOOKS

This is a work of fiction. Names, characters, places and incidents are either the product of the author's imagination or, if real, used fictitiously. All statements, activities, stunts, descriptions, information and material of any other kind contained herein are included for entertainment purposes only and should not be relied on for accuracy or replicated as they may result in injury.

First published in Great Britain 2014 by Walker Books Ltd
87 Vauxhall Walk, London SE11 5HJ

10 9 8 7 6 5 4 3 2 1

Text © 2012 Glenn Wood
Cover illustration © 2014 Craig Phillips

The right of Glenn Wood to be identified as author of this work has been asserted by him in accordance with the Copyright, Designs and Patents Act 1988

This book has been typeset in Adobe Caslon Pro

Printed and bound in Great Britain by Clays Ltd, St Ives plc

British Library Cataloguing in Publication Data:
a catalogue record for this book is available from the British Library

ISBN 978-1-4063-5435-5

www.walker.co.uk

*To my wife Eula, for being my sounding-board, rock and financier;
and to Devon, my daughter/creative consultant (unpaid).*

# PROLOGUE

The shadow on the wall was of a small man with scraggly hair and a long, thin hook-shaped nose. It moved quickly through the city, stretching as its owner passed under streetlamps then shrinking as he scuttled away.

The man was dressed entirely in black. Black shoes, black socks, black jeans, black underwear (not currently on display), a black jacket and black gloves. If he had passed through an X-ray machine, it would have revealed that his heart was also black.

The figure stopped outside a large, modern two-storey house that sat halfway down a leafy suburban street called Success Court. The number

11 was etched into the side of a stainless-steel letter box. The house was bathed in darkness. Both the house and street were quiet and still. The man slipped behind a sculptured bush and crept through impeccably landscaped grounds. He moved to the rear of the property, stopping abruptly as a shaft of moonlight illuminated his reflection in a ground-floor window. He could make out the colour of his eyes: one brown and the other blue. He blinked, then his lips curled into a smile, revealing teeth that were pointed like the incisors of a rat.

He checked the area for movement. Nothing. The yard was empty. The only sound was the tinkle of water cascading into a nearby birdbath.

Stepping back from the window, the figure reached into his belt and removed a radar scanner and a GPS unit. He had designed the device him-self. It would produce a thermal image of the interior of any building it was pointed at, high-lighting the brainwaves of anyone in there. These images were then relayed back to the GPS viewer.

The man examined the house methodically. He could see the brain patterns of two adults asleep in a large bed in a downstairs room. A peanut-shaped blip indicated that a cat slept at the bottom of a set of stairs, and two child-sized signatures were emitted from a bunk bed in an upstairs room.

Placing the scanner and GPS unit back on his belt, he slunk along the side of the house until he stood directly beneath the children's room. The window was partially open.

The man reached for his tool belt once again and withdrew a box about the same size as a block of butter. He put the box under the open window and tapped the lid. It flipped opened with surprising speed, extending lengthways. Then, as if by magic, a ladder appeared and rose into the air. Rung after rung sprang silently from the box until the ladder was tall enough to reach the upstairs window. The man pushed a button on the side of the box and the ladder stopped growing. With a solid clack, the last few rungs snapped into place.

The man began climbing. He moved with the grace of a cat, making no sound. Within seconds he was outside the children's room.

Opening the window a little wider, he studied

the bedroom. It was compact and tidy, dominated by a double-bunk bed. Two boys aged between eight and ten slept soundly under matching superhero blankets. Their rhythmic breathing filled the room. A variety of toys were packed neatly into boxes at the end of the bed and clothing sat clean and folded in two sets of open drawers.

A look of disgust crossed the man's face.

I bet they are good boys, he thought. Well, not for much longer.

A transparent ball about the size of the head of a lollipop appeared in his hand. A purple mist swirled inside. The man squeezed the ball then rolled it onto the bedroom floor. After a few seconds the outer skin of the globe dissolved and the mist leaked into the room.

"That'll make sure you don't wake up."

From beneath his jacket the man withdrew a device that looked like a Thermos flask, except the cylindrical body of the Thermos was made of clear Perspex and it didn't hold tea or coffee. Instead, it contained a minute engine. The man claimed the motor was powerful enough to suck the coat off a wombat, though no one was brave enough to ask him how he knew. Attached to the top of the device were a short fat tube and a suction cup.

Holding the Thermos in one hand, the man reached into his tool belt and took out a gas mask. He placed it on his face and crept further into the mist-filled room.

# ONE

It was a big day for Callum McCullock.

Not only was he turning thirteen, but sitting at the end of his bed was a brand-new jet black Thunderkit X5 All-Terrain wheelchair. He'd wanted a Thunderkit for over a year and his grandmother had finally relented.

Callum needed the wheelchair because he was paralysed from the waist down. He'd been born with a defect in his spinal cord and his legs were completely useless. Well, not completely, Callum often joked, they made his jeans look good.

Swinging out of bed, he grabbed a set of clothes from his bedside drawers, dressed in a hurry and hopped into the new chair.

The Thunderkit was completely different from every other wheelchair he had owned. For one thing it was twice as expensive, but in Callum's eyes it easily justified its cost. It had a five wheel set-up, with two small wheels at the front and a single stabilizing wheel trailing behind two much larger main wheels. Both the front wheels and the trailing wheel contained nitrogen gas shock absorbers and were fully retractable. They were controlled by a digital console on the inside of the left armrest. The retractable wheel design meant that the Thunderkit was equally stable on uphill and downhill rides. All the wheelchair's components were aeronautical grade and, amongst other things, it had a lightweight carbon-fibre moulded seat, toughened "super grip" push rims and a dynamic hand-operated braking system. And, unlike all his other chairs, which seemed like they'd been designed by fashion-challenged science geeks, this one looked cool.

Callum could barely contain his excitement. If his new chair was as good as he hoped, it would make a big difference in his life. When you're stuck in a wheelchair, mobility is everything, and the Thunderkit looked like it could conquer mountains, or at the very least the steps outside the corner shop.

Desperate to test it out, Callum wheeled quickly but quietly out of the house. It was very early and he didn't want to wake his grandmother. He made his way through the tidy cobbled streets of Thanxton, the village he'd lived in since birth, and headed for the steepest hill in town.

Ten arduous minutes later he sat at the top of a steep, grassy slope. He leaned forwards and eyed the almost vertical, dew-covered gradient that lay before him. He drew a deep breath, ran a hand through his short, sandy-brown hair, retracted the Thunderkit's trailing wheel and then pushed hard on the wheel rims, launching the chair down the hill. The wheelchair picked up speed, bucking over the uneven ground. Grunting with effort, Callum fought for control, suddenly swerving right to avoid a pig-shaped rock. He straightened and hung on as the chair careened down the slope, wind whipping against his face, making his eyes stream. As the hill finally flattened out, a deep trench appeared directly in front of the speeding wheelchair. Callum grabbed the left handbrake and squeezed hard. The chair slid sideways, narrowly avoided the rut and juddered to a halt, its knobbly tyres cutting deep grooves in the grass.

Callum's chest thumped with exhilaration. He slapped the side of the Thunderkit, whooped and gave a satisfied nod, a huge grin on his face. He could never have pulled off that manoeuvre in his old wheelchair. He'd tried often enough, and every time it would tip over halfway down and slam him into the dirt.

After he caught his breath Callum rolled onto the pavement and began the uphill slog back home. He moved fast, partly because he liked to feel the burn in his arms (feeling anything is good when you are a paraplegic), but mainly because he didn't want to be late for breakfast. His grandmother disliked tardiness and Callum hated to disappoint her. He loved his grandmother and although she could be a bit strict at times, he knew she was really just a big softie. Not so soft, however, that his breakfast wouldn't end up in the bin if he didn't get a move on, which would be a shame because his grandmother had mad cooking skills.

A few minutes later he was home. Jumping his wheelchair over the kerb, Callum rolled up the ramp to the front door. He grabbed a garden hose, washed the Thunderkit's wheels, wiped them dry with a towel that was attached to the hose reel and went inside. He hurried into the kitchen, his stomach gurgling like a drain.

Rose, Callum's grandmother, stood by the stove, stirring a steaming pot of home-made baked beans. She was an elegant woman in her late somethingties. Her grey hair was cut conservatively and flattered her well-balanced features and she wore a spotless apron over a simple but stylish dress. A sparkle flashed in Rose's sharp blue eyes when she saw Callum, as it always did. She rushed over and gave him a hug.

"Happy Birthday," she said with a smile. "Do you like the chair?"

"It's wicked, Gran. Thank you so much."

"You are very welcome, young man."

Callum broke the hug and gazed longingly at the beans bubbling on the stove. "Will breakfast be long?"

"No. Your timing is perfect."

Rose returned to the stove, spooned the beans onto a plate and brought them to an immaculately set table.

Callum dug right into the food, stuffing a huge forkful into his mouth.

"Slow down, Callum. You're a gentleman, not an animal," tutted Rose. "And get your elbows off the table. Gracious me, where are your manners this morning?"

Callum adjusted his position at the table and selected a daintier forkful of beans. "Sorry, Gran. I'm just really hungry."

"That's still no excuse for rudeness, is it?"

Callum shook his head.

"It's very important to be polite and respectful, Callum. In my opinion, the way we behave is the only thing separating man from beast. Well, that and opposable thumbs."

Callum wasn't about to argue. He knew how important good behaviour was to his grandmother. She had been the headmistress at Thanxton School for forty years and was largely responsible for making the village the courteous place it was. The population was so polite that the village constable would arrest people with a pleasant "Sorry about this". And even the town drunk would say an effusive "Pardon me" after every beer-fuelled belch.

When Callum had finished his breakfast, he asked the same question he asked every year on his birthday: "Have you heard from Mum?"

Rose shook her head.

Cindy, Callum's mother, was the younger of Rose's two daughters. She'd got pregnant at seventeen and handed responsibility for Callum over to Rose from the moment he was born. Cindy wouldn't tell anyone who Callum's father was, and he clearly wanted nothing to do with the child, so the parental duties fell to Rose. Even though she had lost her husband earlier in the year and was still grieving, Rose was more than happy to raise

Callum. It was an arrangement that suited both Rose and her daughter. Cindy was barely capable of looking after herself let alone a child. Besides, she was busy backpacking around the world and showed no interest in returning home. In fact, Cindy had only been in touch once, when Callum was five. She called to ask if she could change his name to "Moon Spirit". Rose refused, to Callum's relief, and they hadn't heard from her since.

"There might be something in the post," said Rose without much hope. "I forgot to check it yesterday afternoon. I'll have a look now."

Callum called, "Doesn't matter if there's not," as his grandmother left the house. He was surprised to find that he meant it. His mother's absence had been painful when he was younger and he often wondered who his father was but, as the years passed, he realized his grandmother was all he needed. She had always been there for him, the only constant in his turbulent life. He knew how difficult it must be for a woman of her age to look after him, especially with his disability, but she had never complained or made him feel like a burden. Quite simply, Callum could not imagine life without his grandmother.

Rose came back into the house with a single letter in her hand. It was in a standard white envelope so Callum knew it wasn't from his mum. Rose opened the letter and scanned its contents before placing it back in the envelope, the colour draining from her face.

"What is it, Gran?"

Rose waved him away. "Nothing," she said unconvincingly.

She put the letter in a drawer and gave Callum a peck on the cheek. "It's just official nonsense. I'll make some calls and everything will be fine. Now scoot or you'll be late for school. And come straight home tonight please."

Rose hustled Callum out of the house. As he left, he couldn't help feeling that his grandmother was keeping something important from him.

After a short trip Callum arrived at the home of Sophie Barnsworth, his best friend.

Sophie was in the workshop of her father's garage, which is where she could be found most mornings. A welding torch glowed orange in her hand and she had almost disappeared behind a shower of sparks. A dirty, oil-stained pair of overalls covered her athletic frame and her shoulder-length chestnut hair stuck out beneath the back of a welder's mask.

When the sparks died away, Callum could see that Sophie was attempting to attach an unfeasibly large engine to the rear of a remote control battle tank. The tank was no longer the standard model you'd buy in a toy store. Sophie had "improved" it. The tank's gun barrel had been reinforced and extended, obviously so it could fire a heavier payload. The body of the tank had also been strengthened, probably to take the strain of its new engine.

Callum waited patiently while the torch flared again, first yellow then blue. Another shower of sparks cascaded around the workshop like a blizzard of fireflies. Once the engine was attached, Sophie turned and lifted the welder's helmet to reveal a pretty face with pale skin and green eyes.

She saw Callum and smiled. "It's the birthday boy! Wow," she said, eyeing the Thunderkit. "Sweet new ride."

Callum smiled back. "Thanks."

Sophie pulled a pocket-sized canvas bag from under the bench and handed it to her friend. "I made you a pressie."

Callum blushed. "You didn't have to do that."

He reached into the bag and removed a black metal torch. The torch had two buttons on the top.

"The first button turns on the light, which has a really powerful LED bulb," said Sophie, excitedly. "Push the second button."

Callum did as he was told and almost dropped the torch when a metre-long metal rod shot out the end and locked into place.

"What's that for?"

"To make it easier for you to reach light switches and stuff," Sophie said with apprehension. She was worried that Callum might think she was implying he was helpless. He could be oversensitive about those kinds of things.

Callum retracted the rod then fired it out again.

He nodded, obviously impressed. "Thanks, Soph. That's gonna be really useful."

Sophie was relieved. She pointed to the bag. "I've put some clips in there so you can attach it to the chair. And I've got you another present, which'll be ready in a couple of days."

Callum opened his mouth to protest, but Sophie silenced him. "I'm doing it, so no arguments, OK, Cal?"

Callum sighed and agreed. "OK." He clipped the torch bag onto the Thunderkit then looked towards the tank. "What's with the armour? Are you thinking of invading a small country?"

"Actually, this isn't a weapon of war." Sophie patted the tank. "It's a weapon of peace."

"Care to explain how that works?" Callum moved closer and examined the gigantic gun barrel with some scepticism.

"The Dudman twins have been chasing Churchill around the backyard with their remote control helicopter. So I'm going to persuade them to stop."

Mr and Mrs Dudman had recently moved

to Thanxton, much to the displeasure of the village. They were an unpleasant couple and had brought their equally obnoxious twin sons, Wayne and Shane, with them. Since arriving, the twins had delighted in tormenting Churchill, the Barnsworths' pet dog, who was a highly strung terrier that barked at its own shadow.

Callum grinned. "You mean you're going to blow their helicopter peacefully out of the sky."

"I'm just going to fire a warning shot. Once they see the awesome power of my modified centurion, that'll be the end of it."

Sophie stroked the tank affectionately. "It's classic military strategy. Show your enemy you have superior fire-power and they back off."

Callum raised his eyebrows unconvinced.

A sudden barrage of barks shattered the solitude of the normally quiet neighbourhood. An irritating buzzing came from the Barnsworths' backyard.

"Come on. It's show time," said Sophie.

With some effort she lifted the tank from the workbench, placed it on the ground and grabbed the remote control unit. She shed her overalls to reveal her school uniform underneath then headed outside.

Callum followed Sophie into the yard. It was a big area surrounded by a low picket fence. A flat lawn was broken by a selection of flowerbeds, trees, shrubs and a kidney-shaped fish pond. Dour concrete gnomes sat around the water's edge. One dangled a fishing pole into the pond.

The Dudman twins stood in the adjoining yard, technically still on their own property. Shane Dudman had a remote control in his hand and was directing the movements of a miniature yellow helicopter that buzzed over the head of Churchill. The little animal ran in confused circles and took mad flying leaps into the air, snapping at the helicopter as it passed.

Sophie called politely to the twins. "Good morning. Would you mind keeping your helicopter away from my dog please? Thank you so much."

Wayne Dudman poked out his tongue. Shane said something that sounded like "Fizzle me pizzle" and continued dive-bombing the dog.

This time the helicopter's rotor blades got so

close to Churchill's tail that they shaved off a few strands of fur. Churchill let out a yelp and ran under a nearby hedge. The twins laughed.

Sophie called to Callum. "You're a witness. I tried to be civil."

"Yep, they're asking for it all right," agreed Callum.

Placing the battle tank on the back lawn, Sophie switched on the remote control.

The tank's massive engine kicked into life with a throaty roar. She steered it into the middle of the yard then swivelled the turret until the cannon tracked the helicopter. The twins stared at the tank in slack-jawed amazement. Their helicopter hovered in midair just inside the Barnsworths' fence.

With her tongue between her teeth, Sophie raised the tank's gun so its gigantic muzzle faced just above the helicopter and pressed the fire button.

*KABLAMO!*

The concussion blast alone was enough to knock the helicopter out of the air. The craft spun end over end, buzzing erratically until it collided with a tree. The impact smashed the helicopter into dozens of pieces. The main rotor blade broke away and spiralled through the air before finally embedding itself in the nose of the fishing gnome. The remainder of its shattered body plummeted to the ground, making a sound like an old car trying to start on a cold morning. It crunched into the grass and sat broken and silent on the ground.

No one even looked at the wreckage. All eyes were on the projectile that had blasted from the tank's gun turret.

Callum shouldn't have been surprised that Sophie's tank fired a miniature ballistic missile, but he was. He had expected a BB pellet or a ball-bearing, not a sleek and deadly rocket with stabilizing fins and an explosive charge in the nose.

And it hadn't finished yet. The rocket hit the upstairs window of the Dudmans' house. There was a blast so loud that Callum could feel the vibration through his chair. In a split second the window was reduced to thousands of wood splinters and twinkling shards of glass. The fragments rained down upon the Dudmans' driveway, covering the concrete with a layer of debris. As the last echoes of the explosion faded away, a roar of fury rose from within the Dudmans' house.

Callum looked at the wreckage open-mouthed. "If that was a warning shot, I'd hate to see what would happen if you really meant it!"

"Hmm," said Sophie. "I may have made some miscalculations."

"You think?"

"Time for school, I reckon." Sophie was already heading out of the yard.

Callum pushed on his rims, caught up to his friend and the two of them disappeared up the road.

# TWO

Callum and Sophie joined a mass of other schoolchildren filing through the gates of Thanxton School.

They were just about to enter when they saw a small boy with bright red hair and a freckly face pushing a damaged bicycle up the road. It was their friend Jinx Patterson. His real name was Toby Patterson but nobody ever called him that, not even his parents. Jinx was way more appropriate, given that bad luck followed him wherever he went.

Callum waved. The boy waved back in a dejected manner and trudged towards them. The front wheel of his bike was badly bent and his clothing was mud stained and dishevelled.

Jinx reached into his schoolbag and withdrew a battered package. He handed it to Callum. "Happy Birthday," he muttered.

Callum shook the package, the contents tinkling brokenly.

"It's a model car, but it may have got a bit crunched in the crash."

Callum and Sophie exchanged a look.

"Another accident, eh, Jinx? How many is that?"

Jinx thought for a minute. "Twenty-seven this year."

"It's only February," gasped Sophie. "What happened this time?"

"Sudden wind gust. Blew me into a drainage ditch."

Callum looked at his friend, concerned. "You OK?"

"Yeah, you know what my luck's like. Bad stuff happens but I never get hurt much. Doesn't do my popularity any good though. Did you guys hear what happened yesterday?"

They shook their heads.

"Some kids actually picked me to play in their rugby team at lunchtime. Just as I was about to score, the goalpost fell over. It knocked the ball out of my hand and smashed Reggie. That'll be the last time anyone has me in their team."

Callum suppressed a grin. "Don't worry. We'll always be your friends. Won't we, Soph?"

"'Course. Bad luck doesn't scare me." Sophie wiped some of the mud off Jinx's jacket. "Come on, we'll be late."

The three friends entered the school grounds and made their way towards the classrooms.

Suddenly, Jinx's thumb began to shake.

"Uh-oh," said Jinx. "Watch out. When bad luck's going to kick in, my thumb starts doing this crazy dance."

Jinx's thumb jerked about like it was trying to escape from his palm. He grabbed it with his other hand and tried to hold it still but it was no good; the thumb kept wriggling like a hyperactive worm.

Callum and Sophie looked around uneasily. "How long's this been going on?" asked Callum.

Jinx continued to battle his thumb. "Just started

recently. Scared the hell out of me the first time it happened, but don't worry – it stops as soon as the bad luck hits."

At that very moment a massive splodge of bird poop fell from the sky and landed on Jinx's head. His thumb immediately stopped shaking. Jinx reached up and patted the splatter that was already beginning to matt his hair. To Callum's and Sophie's surprise, he smiled.

"Phew. It's only bird poo. I thought for a minute that something really horrible was going to happen."

Callum and Sophie left Jinx to clean up and headed for class. English was their first subject and they arrived just before the bell. A crowd of students milled around outside waiting for the lesson to start. The classroom was one of many that didn't have a wheelchair ramp, and three steep steps stood before Callum and the door. Sophie walked behind the Thunderkit and took hold of the rear of Callum's seat, ready to pull him up the stairs, but Callum jerked the wheelchair forwards, breaking her grip.

"Hey," she cried, rubbing her wrist.

Callum spun around, a determined look on his face. "Sorry, but I want to get up by myself. It's a new chair. I can do it."

Sophie stood aside, arms folded tightly across her chest.

The assembled students turned to watch as Callum wheeled his chair up to the first step.

The Thunderkit was fitted with "in and out" adjustable settings. In "out" mode the wheels slanted out from the seat giving the chair width and stability, allowing it to cope with almost any terrain. When "in" mode was selected, the wheels straightened so it could cruise through doorways.

Callum activated the rear wheel, retracted the front wheels and clicked into out mode. He felt the chair drop, then nudged the big wheels closer to the step. Leaning back, he pushed hard on the rims. The chair climbed the first step with ease. Pausing to find his balance, Callum grasped the rims once more. He grunted with effort and pushed forwards. The big wheels bounced up the second step. Just as it looked like he would make it to the top, the rear wheel jammed on the edge of the previous step. Callum lost his balance and the chair tumbled down the steps, tipped over and threw him to the ground. A gasp rippled through the crowd and someone at the back gave a cruel laugh. Sophie glared at the group then ran to Callum's side. She righted the chair and reached down to help him back into it. Callum brushed her away, his face burning with embarrassment and frustration.

"Leave me alone," he snapped.

Sophie retreated.

With considerable effort Callum slowly dragged himself back into the seat. His uniform was dusty and crumpled, and he was breathing heavily.

"Show's over," he growled at the crowd.

The students wandered away, whispering amongst themselves.

Sophie stalked over, leaned in close and hissed into Callum's ear. "You don't have to be so stubborn. We all need help sometimes."

Callum looked away and said nothing.

Sophie grabbed the rear of the chair and pulled

him roughly up the steps. She let go once they'd reached the top and stormed into the classroom. Callum sat where Sophie had left him for a few moments, blinking back angry tears. He wiped his eyes, drew a deep breath then followed her inside.

When the class had finished, Callum rolled over to Sophie and passed her an amusing sketch he'd drawn of her battle tank blowing out the Dudmans' window. Sophie smiled. She knew this was as close to apologizing as Callum would get. He didn't like talking about his disability or how it affected him. He was constantly trying to prove he didn't need help. In fact, Sophie and Rose were the only ones Callum would let touch his chair, and she was worried that the Thunderkit would encourage him to be even more reckless.

The rest of the school day passed slowly. Finally, the bell went and Callum rushed home. He pushed open the door, jumped the jamb and rolled inside.

As soon as he entered, he knew something was wrong. It was after four o'clock and there were no cooking smells in the air. Normally the scent of freshly baked scones or biscuits would fill the room and he'd hear the reassuring sound of a hearty stew bubbling away on the stove. Today there was nothing, literally not a sausage.

Panic rose in Callum's throat like a geyser steaming up from his stomach. Had his grandmother had an accident? He called out, his voice cracking with worry. "Gran, are you OK?"

Rose bustled into the room. She seemed to be fine physically but was in a most uncharacteristic flap. "Gracious me, no."

Rose planted a kiss on his cheek. Callum wiped it away with his hand.

"Sorry, dear. Where are my manners? Good afternoon, young man. How was school?"

"Fine thanks, Gran, but what's going on? You look terrible."

Callum wasn't being rude; his grandmother did look a mess. Her hair slumped to one side, her make-up was smudged and her clothing was rumpled. He had never seen her in such a state.

Rose sighed, walked to the drawer in the kitchen

and withdrew the letter that had arrived in the post. She passed it to Callum. "It's from the Welfare Department. Now that you are thirteen, you are classed as a young adult, and they believe you'll need a higher level of supervision. They think I'm too old to provide it and want to review your case."

"You're not too old. That's rubbish," scoffed Callum.

"Yes, it is, but we have to convince them that I'm still capable of being your guardian. I've been on the phone all day, and they want to see us in person." Rose wrung her hands and added another wrinkle to her dress. "It means we have to go to the city."

All of a sudden Rose's extreme agitation made sense. Callum knew his grandmother hated going to the city. He'd listened to many lectures about what an overcrowded, noisy, polluted and dangerous place it was. Last time Rose was there a rude young man bumped into her on the footpath and knocked her to the ground. Then he carried on walking without a word of apology. To make matters worse, no one had stopped to help her up. Rose also noticed ex-students of hers who moved to the city couldn't be bothered staying in touch, unlike their counterparts in the village who visited her regularly. From this she concluded that everyone in the city was ill-mannered and only interested in themselves. Callum thought she was being a bit harsh but knew better than to contradict his grandmother. He tried to be positive instead.

"It'll be all right, Gran. We'll go to the city together, and I'll convince them you're doing a brilliant job of looking after me. Everything will be fine."

Callum couldn't imagine being taken away from his grandmother; it would be his worst nightmare and he was determined not to let it happen.

Rose calmed slightly. "I suppose." She hesitated, her mind clearly on something else. "The letter got me thinking. I'd like to be more than just your guardian. Your mother has been out of contact for many years now, long enough for me to apply to adopt you." Rose glanced at her grandson and hurried on. "But we don't have to worry about that, if it isn't what you want."

Callum grinned. "Of course it's what I want." He rolled closer to his grandmother and threw his arms around her.

Rose squeezed her grandson, a smile returning to her face. "I'm so pleased. I'll file the papers as soon as I've got this silly interview out of the way."

After a few minutes Callum broke the hug. "They wouldn't really take me away from you, would they?"

His grandmother grew serious. "It's unlikely, but if they did find me unsuitable, they could place you under the guardianship of another relation."

"Like who?"

"Aunt Rebecca," said Rose.

Callum repressed a shudder. Rebecca was Rose's eldest daughter. She had moved to the city many years ago where she married a wet fish of a man called Ken. Callum didn't mind Rebecca; she was a bit of a drama queen but was harmless enough. The problem was her two kids – ten-year-old Mitchell and eight-year-old Bradley. They were loud, obnoxious, hyperactive and generally behaved as if pieces of their brains were missing.

The thought of living with his aunt's brood of monsters was too horrible to contemplate, but Callum pushed his fears aside.

"No one could look after me better than you, and the welfare people will see that. I'm sure of it."

Rose nodded. "Well, I guess we'd better get ready for a trip to the city then. Unfortunately, we'll have to stay with Rebecca." Rose put on a brave face. "Perhaps it won't be as awful as we think."

Callum forced a smile. "It'll be fine."

They both knew it was going to be horrid, but if they'd had even the smallest clue of what was in store, they would have bolted the front door and never left the village.

# THREE

Lester Smythe heaved a heavy sigh. He ran his skinny fingers through his black scraggly hair then scratched his hooked nose. He was standing behind a large, walnut inlaid desk in the plush office of his warehouse lair. Lester owned a successful car parts importing business, which funded his more insidious activities, like being an evil criminal genius. The business gave him an air of respectability and allowed him to hide his other projects from prying eyes.

Lester slammed his fist onto the desk with surprising strength and the two men standing before him jumped.

"Why is this so difficult?" he roared.

Darryl Yarmouth bowed his bald head and stared at his huge feet. He was a giant of a man, more than two metres tall, with a body that looked like it'd been sculpted out of rocks. But still he shuffled nervously and waited for the man beside him to speak.

"It's pretty complicated stuff, Boss," muttered Parson Richie, the other man in the room. Parson was shorter than Darryl but not by much. His frame was lean and he had abnormally long arms. He wore his shoulder-length black hair twisted into dreadlocks.

Lester stalked around to the front of his desk. He pointed to a clear cylindrical flask that lay on the desk. A tube and suction cup were attached to the top of the flask.

"No, it's not," he said as he picked up the flask and waved the suction cup at the two men. "You stick this over the kid's ear, turn on the engine and it sucks the goodness out of their head. The goodness comes out as a pulsating green blob and gets trapped in the flask. Then you quickly screw on the lid so the blob of goodness doesn't escape. Easy-peasy. You'd have to be a moron to mess that up. You're not a moron, are you, Parson?"

Parson shook his head; his dreadlocks waved back and forth like seaweed in a tidal pool. He was scared of Lester, partly because of Lester's weird eyes (one was blue and the other brown), but mainly because the man was a psychotic lunatic.

Darryl held up a baseball-sized hand, as if he was still in school. "I'm still not sure why we're doing it."

"You don't have to be," snarled Lester. "You just have to do what I tell you."

Lester stared at Darryl until the big man looked away. He had no intention of explaining to his henchmen why he detested goodness and wanted to rid the world of it.

His mind drifted back to his first day at Jacktown Primary School in the city. He'd arrived in a taxi, his mother was too busy drinking gin to drop him off. He stared at the big building he was supposed to enter, took a deep breath then pushed his way through the crowds of children being hugged by teary-eyed parents. He made it through the first half of the day by staying out of everyone's way, ignored at school almost as much as he was at home. Then came lunchtime. He entered the school cafeteria, grabbed a plate and stepped in front of a long queue of hungry children. Lester didn't realize he was doing anything wrong; his parents hadn't let him mix with other kids or bothered to teach him how to behave properly. This mattered little to the large, red-faced officious man who grabbed his arm and pulled him from the queue.

"It seems we have a dirty little queue jumper," bellowed the man, who turned out to be Jacktown Primary's principal. "Don't you have any manners, boy?"

Lester struggled to free himself from the man's grip, but he was held too tightly. He was aware that every person in the cafeteria had stopped what they were doing, watching him. His cheeks burned.

The man repeated himself. "I asked you if you had any manners, you vile child. Answer me."

Lester didn't know what to say so he said

nothing. Tears of confusion and embarrassment stung his eyes.

His silence enraged the big man whose face changed from red to purple. The man grabbed a pad and a black marker and wrote the words "I'm a bad boy" on a piece of paper, then taped it to Lester's chest. He lifted Lester off the ground and placed him on a desk next to the lunch queue. The man roared to the watching crowd. "I want you all to take a good look at this ill-mannered troublemaker. This rude fellow will eat lunch last for the rest of the term." The man then stood beside Lester to make sure he stayed on the desk.

As the line of sniggering, pointing children filed past him, Lester vowed revenge on all of them. "If you say I'm bad, then I will be," he swore.

Lester didn't go back to that school (which mysteriously burned down the following week), but the mocking laughter of the supposedly good children was etched into his brain. It was the beginning of a lifelong hatred of society and its accepted rules of behaviour. By his early teens

Lester found that any display of goodness was physically repugnant to him. On one occasion he actually threw up because he saw a teenager on a bus give his seat to an old lady.

At age twenty, Lester focused his considerable intelligence on one goal – designing a machine that could suck the goodness clean out of a person's head. Six months later he created the Mark One Brain Sucker. Unfortunately, it had a significant flaw. It sucked out the goodness no problem at all, but it took half the brain as well. Lester discovered this side effect when his first test subject woke up as a foul-mouthed, blithering idiot. Ironically, the man went on to have a successful career as a school principal.

After this hiccup Lester decided to concentrate his efforts on children. He did some rather unpleasant tests that are, frankly, too disturbing to describe and discovered that the goodness in children wasn't yet fully formed and hadn't spread throughout the brain. Instead it clustered together in a living, pulsating green mass near the frontal lobe. This was great news for Lester as it would make the goodness much easier to extract.

Armed with this information, Lester invented the Mark Two Brain Sucker. This machine was a vast improvement on the Mark One. It sucked the goodness out but left the brain intact. And except for a craving for fried onions, it had no side effects at all.

Lester had been sucking the goodness from the kids of the city for fifteen years now and was growing impatient with his progress. Sure, a lot of the kids who'd been brain sucked were growing up to be rude and spiteful adults. And he was pleased to see they were making the city a thoroughly unpleasant place, but it was all happening too slowly for Lester. At the rate he was going he would never complete his goal of eradicating goodness from the world. He needed help, which was why he was attempting to school his henchmen in the art of brain sucking.

He placed the Mark Two Brain Sucker on the desk and turned to Darryl and Parson. "Any more stupid questions?"

They shook their heads.

Lester passed the brain sucker to Darryl. "Right then, practise on Parson."

"No way." Parson backed away in fear and held up his long arms.

Lester grinned and took a child's doll out of his desk drawer. "I was kidding. Use this."

He tossed the doll to Darryl who caught it in his huge hands, then tried to attach the suction cup to its ear. He snapped the doll's head right off.

Lester sighed. "We want to suck out their goodness – not kill them."

Darryl tried again. This time he dropped the doll. Then he dropped the Thermos. Then he dropped the doll *and* the Thermos.

After watching Darryl mess it up seven times in a row, Lester gave up. "As you seem to have the dexterity of a concrete block, your job on this mission will be lookout. Clearly you are useless at everything else."

Darryl looked hurt. Parson felt sorry for him. "He could release the knockout gas, Boss."

Darryl looked at Lester hopefully.

"All right," Lester conceded. "Even a trained monkey couldn't mess that up."

He pulled a purple globe out of his desk and carefully passed it to Darryl. Lester pointed to a parking garage that adjoined his office.

He was going to say, "When I give you the signal, squeeze the ball gently, then roll it into the garage," but he didn't get a chance. Darryl took the ball in his huge hand and immediately crushed it. Purple knockout gas spewed from his palm. Ten seconds later, Lester, Parson and Darryl fell unconscious onto the office floor.

# FOUR

Callum woke the morning before the trip with a brilliant idea. He flipped off his bed into his wheelchair and raced to his grandmother's room, stopping in the doorway.

His grandmother sat fully dressed in front of her mirror, immaculately groomed once again. Callum watched as she brushed her grey hair in short, even strokes and waited for her to notice him.

Rose saw him in the mirror and smiled. "Come in, Callum. Did you sleep well?"

Callum rolled over to her. "Yes, thank you, Gran. Can I ask you something?"

"Certainly, go ahead."

Callum hesitated. He had to phrase this exactly right.

"You know how tomorrow we're going to the city. I was thinking how much easier it would be for you if we brought Soph and Jinx along." Callum didn't give his grandmother a chance to respond before launching into the rest of his pitch.

"They can help with my wheelchair and with navigating around the city. They'll be no trouble. They're really quiet, and Soph's great with kids so the three of us will be able to keep Mitchell and Bradley out of your hair. And we've still got a few days of school holidays left. Can they come? Can they?"

"So you think they'll be helpful, do you?"

Callum nodded so hard his head nearly fell off.

With a wry smile, his grandmother stood and headed towards the kitchen. "Well, I suppose a couple of extra hands could be useful."

Rose stopped at the refrigerator and pulled out some eggs for breakfast. Callum waited patiently for her to continue.

"If their parents agree, then it's fine by me."

"Thanks, Gran. I'll go ask them." Callum gave his grandmother a quick hug then spun his wheelchair and headed out the door.

Rose called him back. "Might I suggest you get dressed first?"

Callum glanced down and blushed. He was still in his pyjamas.

He got dressed in a flash and was at Sophie's house twenty minutes later. Callum found his friend in the workshop as usual, listlessly dismantling the battle tank.

"I take it you're not doing that voluntarily," he said.

"No," muttered Sophie as she removed the engine. "The Dudmans are still on the warpath and this is part of my punishment."

"Shame. It was a great tank."

Sophie nodded. "I can't come outside either. My parents want me to keep a low profile."

"I think I can help with that."

Callum explained the trip to Sophie.

Her eyes lit up. "That'd be great. I'll go and ask Mum."

Sophie rushed out of the garage and returned soon after with permission to go.

"They thought me going away was a brilliant idea." She paused. "Should I be worried that my parents looked relieved when I asked to leave town for a few days?"

Callum laughed. "Worried, yes. Surprised, no. I'll go and see Jinx then tell Gran the good news."

Sophie went back to the bench. "OK, cool. I'll put a kit together for the city."

Callum wasn't sure what she meant, but it made him very nervous. He chewed on Sophie's comments all the way to Jinx's house, but then let it drop. He guessed he'd find out what her city kit looked like soon enough.

Arriving at Jinx's place, he was surprised, as he always was, to find the house still standing. It had probably been an ordinary two-storey home once – before the Pattersons, or more specifically Jinx, moved in. Now it looked like a disaster area (which in many ways it was). The roof was a patchwork of old and new tiles, where it had been repaired over and over again due to being struck by everything from lightning to giant hailstones and probably the odd meteorite. The walls leaned slightly to the left, and the whole house sagged on its battered foundations.

Callum squelched up the sodden path to the front door. A flash flood had engulfed their yard (and only *their* yard) a few days earlier, which was strange because there hadn't been any rain in Thanxton for several months. Callum rang the doorbell, which gave one last pathetic *bing bong* before exploding. Jinx answered the door. He glanced at the smoking remains of the doorbell. "You're a witness. I didn't do that."

Callum smiled. "Don't worry, mate. I'll back you up."

"I get blamed for everything that goes wrong around here. And really, I'm only responsible for about eighty per cent of it, maybe eighty-five."

"Rough day, eh?"

"They're all rough days," Jinx said with a shrug. "Do you want to come in?"

Callum shook his head. "Nah, it's cool. I just wondered if you'd like to come on a trip to the city with me and Soph tomorrow?"

Jinx brightened. "I'd love to come." But as soon as his mood lifted, it dropped again. "Darn it. I can't; I'm grounded. Someone put wasabi in my sister's Marmite sandwiches." He called loudly back into the house so his parents could hear. "It could have been some sort of freak accident."

Callum was appalled. "Man, that sucks. Getting punished for your bad luck."

Jinx grinned and dropped his voice to a whisper. "Actually, I did it. My sister's really annoying."

Callum laughed. "Marmite and wasabi! Genius."

"Yeah, it was pretty funny. She spat sandwich all over the cat. Bummer about tomorrow though; I'd have enjoyed that. Thanks for thinking of me, Cal."

"'Course," said Callum. "We're mates, aren't we?"

"Yeah," he replied. Then after Callum had gone, Jinx shut the door and added quietly to himself, "That's what I'm thanking you for."

Sophie arrived at Callum's house bang on time the following morning. Both she and Rose were disappointed Jinx couldn't make it. Sophie carried a suspiciously large blue sports bag and Callum had to stop himself from grilling her about what was inside.

Ten minutes later the kids had loaded their gear into Rose's big, old sky-blue Volvo. Before they left, Sophie politely asked Rose to flip the hood so she could see "what that baby was packing". Before Rose could stop her, she'd cleaned the spark plugs, replaced the air filter and adjusted the timing.

The journey to the city was uneventful. Rose was a cautious driver, and she kept firmly to the speed limit. Shortly after leaving Thanxton, the rolling green fields of the countryside gave way to a less pleasant landscape. The trees thinned out then disappeared altogether, replaced by squat warehouses and ugly grey factories that belched plumes of smoke into the air.

Rose grew quiet as the birdsong vanished and

was exchanged with the swish of passing cars. During the ride through the countryside she had chatted almost continuously. Now she hardly said a word.

Callum broke the silence. "Do we go into the city centre, Gran?"

Rose nodded. "Yes, that's where the welfare office is."

Sophie squirmed in her seat, fascinated by the variety of cars that zoomed past. "What's the middle of the city like?" she asked, eyes shining with excitement.

"You'll soon see for yourself," said Rose.

The car reached the top of a hill and the vista changed. Sprawled out before them lay the heart of the city. Sunlight glinted off the many windows of the huge glass towers that dominated the skyline, each building trying to outdo its neighbour in terms of height and grandeur. Every now and then a patch of green interrupted the gleaming metal as parks, a zoo and a football stadium came into view. Both Sophie and Callum thought it was quite a beautiful sight, but wisely chose not to mention this to Rose.

As they closed in on the big glass buildings, the streets got narrower and more crowded. Callum noticed that Sophie withdrew from the window as the streets became more congested, her initial excitement replaced by a look of concern. The blare of a car horn distracted him before he could say anything.

Vehicles now flew at the Volvo from every direction. Rose reacted to the increased traffic by hunching down into her seat and gripping the steering-wheel so hard her knuckles grew white. The car's speed dropped to a crawl, which caused more horn tooting and arm waving. An angry woman in a shiny silver BMW flicked a rude sign at Rose and a massive truck pulled right up behind them, its grille almost touching their bumper. A red sports car zoomed past on the inside, its side mirror clipping the Volvo's mirror, breaking it with a sharp crack. Sophie checked the fastenings on their seat belts.

"Why are they all driving so close?"

Rose's voice was tight and clipped. "Because they have no manners."

Callum pointed to a fat, bald middle-aged man sitting in a car just opposite them at a set of lights. He was pounding on his steering-wheel with his fists and his face had gone a strange purple colour.

"Look," said Callum. "That man's head's about to explode."

Sophie laughed. A tiny smile cracked Rose's grim demeanour.

"Keep your eyes open for a parking space, children."

Callum saw a car pull away from the kerb just ahead of them and called to his grandmother. "There's one."

Rose pressed her indicator and moved towards the parking space. She drove past the gap, stopped and began reversing into it. Suddenly, a small car with a big exhaust pipe broke from the traffic and swerved, nose first, into Rose's parking space. Callum and Sophie were thrown forwards in their seats as Rose stamped on the brakes. The Volvo's rear end was almost touching the front of the other car. This was too much for Rose. She tooted her horn and turned around to glare at the other driver. A teenage boy emerged from the car. He was dressed in a baggy T-shirt and shorts that were several sizes too large for him. The shorts hung halfway down his backside, showing off a pair of purple satin boxer shorts. A baseball cap sat on his head, twisted sideways so the peak sat over his left ear. He looked directly at Rose and pointed at her, making the shape of a gun with his fingers and cocked his thumb in a firing motion. He then spat a lump of chewing-gum onto the road and walked away.

Callum and Sophie looked at each other open-mouthed. They had never seen such bad behaviour.

"And that," Rose said with a sigh, "is why I hate coming to the city."

Half an hour later Rose finally found a parking space. The problem now was getting to the office building. The streets were teeming with pedestrians and becoming more congested by the minute.

Sophie stared nervously at the throng. "I've never seen so many people."

Something in her tone made Callum spin around. His friend's eyes were wide and her face was flushed. "Are you all right?" he asked.

Sophie clasped and unclasped her hands. "Yeah, yeah, I'm fine."

Rose studied the girl for a moment before speaking gently. "Sophie, are you claustrophobic?"

"Sometimes," Sophie answered quietly. "I don't like big crowds or tight spaces."

Callum was amazed. He'd never known Sophie to be afraid of anything.

His grandmother made a quick decision. "Sophie will stay here and guard the car. Callum and I will hurry into the office and be back in no time. OK?"

Sophie gave a slight, embarrassed nod.

Callum patted her arm. "It's cool."

Sophie didn't reply. She couldn't take her eyes off the busy street.

As Callum and Rose made their way to the welfare office, Callum thought how lucky Sophie was to be in the car. The crowds had worsened and no matter how loudly he or his grandmother yelled "Excuse me", people kept bumping into them. A very thin and smartly dressed woman walked straight into Callum's chair. Her solid leather briefcase smashed into his head. "Watch where you're going," shrieked the woman as she examined her briefcase for damage. She kicked his wheelchair then stormed off. Callum watched her go, dumbfounded.

After much jostling they arrived at the bottom of a flight of stairs that led to the offices of the Welfare Department. Callum was amazed the building wasn't wheelchair friendly. Rose gave a cluck of annoyance then turned Callum around and slowly began to work the Thunderkit up the steps. Dozens of people passed the old lady struggling with the wheelchair and not one of them offered to help.

Rose stopped to catch her breath when they reached the top of the stairs. "Gracious," she said between gasps of air, "I think the behaviour here is even worse than it was last time I visited."

"Perhaps we've just caught them on a bad day."

Rose patted his arm. "That's probably it," she said, admiring his positive attitude.

Signing the forms was just as traumatic as getting to the office. A stick-thin, sour welfare officer plonked a series of legal documents in front of Rose. She wore the expression of someone who just had a bug fly up their nose.

"Extended guardianship and then adoption," she snapped. "Sign these."

Rose read each document very carefully before signing them. She chose to ignore the welfare officer who clicked her tongue impatiently. When Rose had finished, the woman ran a cold gaze over Callum. He felt like a beetle being watched by a hungry spider.

"This is the individual in question?" she asked Rose.

His grandmother nodded.

"I take it he has ... special needs."

The way she said it made Callum angry. It was as if she thought he was stupid. He was about to say something when his grandmother shot him a warning look. Rose leaned very close to the social worker and looked her square in the eye.

"Callum is a very clever boy who is doing exceptionally well in school. As for his physical needs, I have fitted my house with a wheelchair ramp and widened the doorways, something you should probably do here."

The woman held Rose's gaze for a few seconds then backed away.

"And how old are *you*?"

Rose stiffened. "Old enough to know that you don't break up a loving family."

The woman's mouth curled briefly into a cynical sneer, then she brought the interview to an end.

"One of my colleagues will visit your home in three days' time at exactly 8 a.m. She will examine your living conditions and conduct a final interview. If you are found to be unsuitable, the boy will be removed from your care and placed elsewhere. Is that clear?"

Rose smiled politely. "Crystal. Thank you so much."

The welfare officer grabbed the files and swept from the room without another word.

Rose let out a shuddering sigh and patted Callum on the arm. "Let's get out of here."

Callum thought that was the best idea he'd heard all day.

# FIVE

Thirty minutes and five near accidents later, they sat in the driveway of Callum's aunt's house at 11 Success Court. Sophie's mood had brightened as soon as they left the crowds behind, and she was back to her normal confident self.

"Nice place," she said, running an appreciative eye over the impressive home.

Rose tutted. "Yes, but look at the state of the garden."

An assortment of toys were strewn all over the property. An expensive bicycle lay carelessly abandoned in the driveway, and the tip of a skateboard peeked out from underneath a sculptured bush.

Rose took a deep breath and got out of the car. She and Sophie helped Callum into his chair. Then, with some apprehension, they approached the front door.

After pressing the bell, they heard what sounded like a war cry, followed by running footsteps and a crash. Rose gave Callum a nervous look.

A harassed woman in her early thirties opened the door. She wore expensive clothing that had been designed to make the wearer appear casual and relaxed. It wasn't working. She was tall and thin like Rose but had bags under her eyes and looked tired.

Rebecca Kinley (nee McCullock) kissed her mother. "You guys had better come in. I can't leave them alone for long."

A loud smash came from within the house. The woman flinched. "Things are a bit hectic. The boys found some fizzy drink I was hiding and have guzzled a litre of lemonade."

Sophie and Callum exchanged glances. That didn't sound good.

The trail of discarded toys continued indoors.

"Sorry about the mess," said Rebecca as she stepped over a miniature tyrannosaurus rex.

The living-room looked like a bomb had exploded there. Several items of furniture had been tipped over, fast-food wrappers littered the floor and the curtains were torn off their rails. A sliding door leading to the backyard was half open.

The mess was bad enough, but the noise was worse. An Xbox game cycled through a violent opening sequence on the TV, with the volume on full. At the same time an iPod played children's songs through a high-powered stereo, competing with the TV.

All of a sudden two children leaped from behind an upturned couch and ran screaming at the stunned visitors. At first Callum thought they were demons. Ugly slashes of black and red face paint marked their faces. The paint hadn't been applied with any artistic integrity. It was just smeared on. The older of the two was of medium height and weight for a ten-year-old boy. This was Mitchell. He had crafty eyes and brown hair styled to form a ridge on the top of his head.

Bradley, his brother, was the fatter of the two. If Mitchell's eyes were sneaky, then Bradley's were greedy. His hair was close cropped and made his chubby face look even fatter. Both boys wore stained T-shirts and shorts.

The two boys were moving quickly, then they stopped just short of Rose, but continued to yell, "RRRAAAARRRRRGGGGGGGG."

"Quieten down, boys," their mother said ineffectually.

Finally, they ran out of air and stopped screaming. The older boy pointed at Sophie.

"Who are you?"

Sophie was taken aback by the abrupt question.

"I'm Sophie. Didn't anyone tell you it's rude to point?"

Mitchell glared at her, defiant. "Yeah, Mum did, but we ignored her. She's stupid."

Bradley kicked his mother in the ankle, and the two boys ran off laughing. They disappeared into the backyard slamming the sliding door as they went.

Rebecca hobbled to the upside-down couch

and located a remote control unit. She switched off the Xbox and the iPod. Peace descended on the room. Rebecca began turning the furniture back over. Rose and Sophie went to help.

Rose's expression was grim. "Rebecca, I don't want you to take this the wrong way, but the boys…"

Rebecca shook her head and interrupted her mother. Her lips thinned. "I know what you're going to say. But they're really good kids. They're just going through a difficult stage. They don't have any friends at school and no one wants to play with them any more."

Rose said nothing.

Rebecca carried on. "I've tried reasoning with them, but they don't listen. Besides, they're not really bad, just a bit boisterous, that's all."

A football hit the sliding door with a solid thump, causing Sophie to jump. The glass rattled. Bradley ran over to retrieve the ball and looked into the living-room. He pulled a face at Rose and poked out his tongue.

Rebecca ignored her son and wiped her hands on her designer trousers.

"Now, who'd like a drink of juice and some biscuits?" she said with forced cheerfulness.

A little later Sophie, Rose and Callum unpacked the car and were shown to their bedrooms. Callum and Rose were sharing a room on the second floor next to Mitchell and Bradley. Sophie was placed in a separate bedroom just across the hall. Rebecca and Ken slept downstairs.

Callum waited until his grandmother took her afternoon nap, then crossed the hallway and knocked lightly on the door to Sophie's room.

She was busting to talk.

"That was incredible! They are the worst behaved kids I've ever seen in my life. Could you imagine living with them?" Sophie said.

Callum shook his head. "I don't even want to think about it."

"And their mother just lets them get away with it all."

"I know. If I'd behaved like that, Gran would have grounded me until I was twenty."

"I bet they'll be in trouble when their dad comes home."

Callum made sure the door was shut and wheeled his chair closer to Sophie. He lowered his voice. "I doubt it. Their father's as soft as a three-week-old banana. You wait until dinner tonight. They'll be twice as bad."

Sophie's blue bag sat on the end of her bed. She opened it, reached inside and drew out a well-equipped toolkit.

"Do you think your gran would approve of us teaching your cousins a lesson in good manners?"

Callum looked carefully at Sophie. "Why? What do you have in mind?"

Sophie gave a slight shrug and did her best to look innocent. "Oh, nothing much."

He noticed she had changed her clothes and was wearing a skirt. That's weird, he thought, she never wears skirts.

Sophie sat on the end of the bed with her knees pressed primly together. She waved Callum over and told him to sit with his wheelchair facing her. Callum did as he was told, not sure what to expect.

"Watch this," Sophie said. "Let's pretend you

are one of your cousins and have done something incredibly rude."

Sophie looked at him sweetly, then twitched her shoulder.

Suddenly, a wooden spoon attached to the end of a long flexible shaft shot out from under Sophie's skirt. The spoon snapped out, smacked Callum across the lower leg then disappeared back under the fabric.

Callum recoiled with surprise. "What the…"

Callum hadn't actually felt the smack because of his paralysis, but he knew from the crack of the spoon that it would have really stung.

Sophie turned so she could show Callum her invention. She pulled her skirt up just above her knee and revealed that she had a device strapped to the outside of her right thigh.

"I call this 'the spoon of retribution'. I've attached a wooden spoon to a spring-loaded rod. Once the spoon is locked in position, I can fire it by squeezing a pressure pad I've rigged under my armpit. Then the spring fires the rod and *whack* – instant justice."

Callum was fascinated. "How'd you get the spoon to move in a smacking motion?"

"Simple. I put a track in so the rod would take off on an angle. When it's fully extended, it snaps back in line then retracts. And best of all, when I fire it, my hands are above the table. So I couldn't possibly have hit anyone."

Callum laughed. "You're an evil genius."

"Nah, it's just simple physics."

"It's pretty cool, but you can only use it if they really deserve it, OK?"

Sophie smiled innocently. "Of course."

Later that afternoon they met Ken. He was exactly as Callum remembered. His hair was lank and floppy. He looked permanently nervous and spoke so softly it was hard to hear him. When Callum shook his hand, it was like squeezing a marshmallow. Even his clothes were insipid.

As Ken and Sophie talked, the two boys bounced up and down on the living-room furniture, firing spit balls at each other. Their father did nothing.

Before long, dinner was served. It was an

impressive spread – chicken casserole accompanied by new potatoes, corn on the cob and green beans. Several loaves of crusty bread sat on cutting boards beside the food. The meal was placed in the middle of the table so people could help themselves.

Once they had sat down, Rose asked if she could say grace. Rebecca pretended they always did, but the confused looks on her boys' faces suggested otherwise. Not only did the boys not say grace, but they also helped themselves to the food while Rose spoke.

Sophie looked at Callum, obviously hoping to get his permission to unleash the spoon. He shook his head.

Mitchell and Bradley piled their plates with food before anyone else had a chance.

"What did I tell you boys about waiting for our guests?" Rebecca said, a little too late.

Mitchell shrugged. "First in, fullest tummy, eh, Bradley?" he said with his mouth full of food.

Bradley sniggered.

Ken said nothing. He sat at the end of the table

with his head down, avoiding everyone's eyes.

Callum watched his grandmother carefully. She remained silent, but Callum could tell she was biting her tongue.

The trouble really began when Sophie reached for the salt shaker, which sat in the middle of the table. Just as she was about to take hold of it, Mitchell leaned across and grabbed the shaker first. Rose's eyes narrowed, and Sophie stiffened, while Ken and Rebecca pretended not to see.

Callum let out a groan. He waited for the smack of the spoon, but surprisingly Sophie did nothing. She withdrew her hand and waited for Mitchell to finish. Mitchell made a big show of taking an inordinately long time to shake the salt over his food. He had a big grin on his face. Callum noticed a tick developing in the corner of Sophie's eye. She looked across the table at Mitchell.

"May I have the salt, please?"

Mitchell ignored her. Bradley tittered.

Sophie spoke louder this time. "May I have the salt, please?"

Rebecca looked imploringly at her son. The

boy relented and passed the salt to Sophie, but he wasn't finished yet. When Sophie took the shaker, Mitchell refused to let go of the bottom, and a tug-of-war began. Enough was enough. Sophie glanced at Callum, and he nodded.

Sophie's left arm twitched and Callum let out a loud cough, hoping to cover the sound of the spoon hitting Mitchell's leg. His timing was perfect, and the snap of wood meeting skin was barely audible.

He may not have heard it, but Mitchell certainly felt it. He leaped from his chair like a scalded cat and screamed in pain, tears welling in his eyes. His mother looked at him in surprise.

"Mitchell, what's the matter?"

Mitchell pointed at Sophie. "She hit me."

Sophie sat quietly on the other side of the table with her hands folded neatly in front of her, an angelic look on her face.

Rebecca was angry now. "Don't be ridiculous. Both her hands are on the table."

"She kicked me then."

"She's too far away, and I'm sure a nice girl

like Sophie wouldn't dream of doing anything like that."

"Of course not, Mrs Kinley," said Sophie, her voice dripping with honey.

"She did, she did," blubbed Mitchell.

Rebecca looked at her mother and registered the disgust in Rose's eyes. She had no option but to act. "I've just about had enough of you, young man. Straight to bed right now, and no dessert."

Mitchell's jaw dropped. "But…"

Rebecca stood up. "No arguments. Bed this instant. Isn't that right, Ken?"

Rebecca's husband looked about as comfortable as a man who had fallen into a thistle bush in his pyjamas. He blinked twice. His voice quavered. "That's right. Listen to your mother."

Mitchell stared at his parents in disbelief. Quite clearly, he was hardly ever sent to bed early, and never without dessert. He gave them an imploring look, but his gaze was met with a steely resolve. He was beaten, and he knew it. Mitchell threw one last withering glare at Sophie and then limped off to his bedroom.

Bradley watched him go, astonished. He sat quietly in his chair not wanting to follow his brother.

The rest of the meal passed in welcome silence and dessert was brilliant.

## SIX

Lester stood alone in a large laboratory in the underground level of his warehouse lair. He walked over to a toughened glass tank that had been built into the wall. The tank was huge, spanning the length of the room from floor to ceiling. It was filled with thousands of litres of water.

He tapped the glass and grinned as a little, bright green creature jerked with surprise then swam away from the noise.

Contained in the tank were the tens of thousands of blobs of goodness that Lester had stolen from the children of the city. They floated in the water like an assortment of lime octopuses, except they didn't have tentacles. To move about, they expanded and contracted their sleek bodies.

Lester watched as the blobs circled the tank, pulsing with energy while they searched for a way to escape. He held a remote control in his hand and pushed a button labelled "Hunt". A concealed trapdoor opened in the bottom of the tank and a clear tube shaped like a torpedo burst into the water. The curved front of the tube opened and it sped towards one of the floating blobs, sluicing water as it went. The terrified blob tried to dodge away, but the torpedo was too fast. The small green being was sucked into the tube, and the lid snapped shut, trapping it inside. The torpedo then returned to its entry point and dropped into a chute below the trapdoor, which rapidly closed.

Lester moved to a large bench at the far end of his laboratory and pushed a second button on the remote. This one was marked "Display". A section of the bench slid aside with a hiss, and the torpedo containing the green blob was lifted into the air by a robotic arm. The outer skin of the blob rippled with energy as it pressed against the edge of the tube, trying to escape.

Lester picked up a Dictaphone from the bench, pressed record and spoke calmly into the microphone.

"Goodness disintegration experiment number two hundred and twelve. Energy bolt."

Lester walked to the other end of the bench and picked up a weapon that looked like a cross between a high-powered rifle and a flame thrower. He pulled a power cord from the weapon's stock and plugged it into a wall socket. The weapon emitted a high-pitched hum then began to beep. Lester put on a pair of protective goggles then aimed the gun at the torpedo tube. He pulled the trigger, and a bright blue bolt of energy blasted from the barrel and smashed into the torpedo tube blowing it into a thousand pieces. A silver ripple flashed momentarily along the surface of the blob's skin, repelling the electrical charge, then it fell to the bench, green and wriggling.

Cursing, Lester wrenched off his goggles and picked up a large glass jar. He strode down the length of the bench and slammed the jar over the blob before it could scuttle away. He picked up his Dictaphone and growled into it.

"Disintegration failed. Energy bolt unable to penetrate protective field."

Lester stomped over to the tank wall and banged on the glass in frustration, causing a mass of green blobs to scatter away. He'd tried shooting, stabbing, burning, exploding and even poisoning to destroy them, but so far his experiments had failed. He could catch the blobs, but he couldn't kill them. Which meant if they ever escaped, they'd make their way back to their owners, slip back into their heads and restore their goodness. Then all his work would have been for nothing.

He returned to his workstation, turned on his computer and began trawling the Internet. The answer was out there somewhere. He just had to find it.

"I had a visitor earlier," said Sophie, when Callum crept into her room. "Mitchell waited until his parents were out of earshot then opened my door and hissed at me."

Callum sniggered. "What did he say?"

"He said, 'I know you did it and I'm gonna get you back. You, my stupid cousin and old stiff knickers. You'll all pay'," said Sophie, doing a fair impression of Mitchell the Moron. "Then he slammed the door and stomped away before I could reply."

As she spoke, she withdrew a large plastic bag from her luggage and tipped the contents onto the bedspread. A set of nose plugs, a length of rope, a walkie-talkie, a smoke bomb, camouflage paint and a dart gun lay on the bed.

"What's all this for?" asked Callum with a note of concern.

"If Mitchell and Bradley are planning a revenge attack, I thought we should be prepared."

Callum ran a critical eye over the equipment. "A dart gun?"

"I've adapted it so it fires a sticky ball of gum containing an audio tracking bug. It'll give us their exact location, and if we are within fifty metres, we should be able to hear them as well."

"I'm glad you're on my side."

Sophie smiled. "Hide in here with me and we can ambush them. They're most likely to attack me first. I'm the one who whacked him, and I'm just a defenceless girl."

Callum watched Sophie as she dug around in her toolkit. He couldn't think of anyone less defenceless.

Darryl and Parson cruised the city streets in a black van with darkened windows. They were out on their very first solo brain-sucking mission and were determined nothing would go wrong. Convincing Lester to let them go hadn't been easy. He was still unhappy about the gassing incident, but breaking one of Darryl's fingers with a book entitled *Effective Management Techniques* had improved his mood, and he relented.

Darryl rested his heavily bandaged finger on the top of the steering-wheel as he drove.

He swung the van into a quiet city suburb.

Parson sat in the passenger seat. He played the goodness scanner over the houses, trying to find a suitable target. The scanner's screen glowed red, indicating that no goodness was present.

Parson scowled. "Nothin'. The boss has sucked the place dry."

Darryl shifted impatiently in his seat. "He can't 'ave done the whole city."

Right then two green dots and a single golden light blinked on the screen. The signals were so intense that the entire cab was bathed in an emerald glow.

Parson jumped with excitement. "We've got a coupla live ones."

"Where?"

"I'm just triangulating it." Parson swivelled his body so Darryl couldn't see. His face wrinkled in concentration. He had no idea how to triangulate anything, but he wasn't going to admit that to Darryl.

Parson pointed to a large two-storey house – 11 Success Court. "Signal's coming from there."

Darryl parked the van across the road from the

house. He reached into the back seat and grabbed the platinum case that contained the brain sucker then handed it to Parson. "Let's steal us some goodness," he said with a grin.

The two thugs pulled dark green overalls on top of their clothes and put on black balaclavas. They checked their equipment, which included the scanner, knockout globes, gas masks and the brain sucker, then crept up the driveway and broke into the house. Once inside Parson switched the scanner on again. A peanut-shaped blip appeared at the bottom of the stairs. "Cat," said Parson. "Nothin' to worry 'bout."

Two red dots flashed downstairs. "Parents," he said with a nod at the lights.

Darryl grabbed a knockout globe from the case. "I'll sort 'em out."

He quietly opened the door to Rebecca and Ken's room, rolled the globe onto the carpet and closed the door. He waited until he could see tendrils of purple mist seeping under the door then rejoined his partner.

"Job done."

Parson scanned the rest of the house. Two green lights shone in an upstairs bedroom. A golden light pulsed from another upstairs room. Darryl pointed to it. "What's that?"

Parson shook the scanner. "I dunno. I saw it earlier. I thought it was just a glitch."

The golden light radiated bright and strong.

Uncertainty gnawed at Parson. "I think we should call the boss."

"Yeah. A golden light, man. It's gotta be important."

Parson pulled a mobile phone from his pocket and dialled.

Back in his warehouse lair Lester had just typed the words "Goodness destruction" into Google and pressed search. There weren't many hits. He was scanning the pages when the ringtone on his mobile phone played. It was Darth Vader's theme from *Star Wars*. He gave the phone an irritated glare and answered it.

Lester could hear Parson's voice through the tinny speaker. He listened to what Parson had to say, his heart rate increasing as his henchman spoke.

He replied with a forceful voice. "I don't care how you do it, but get me whatever it is that's making the golden glow on the scanner. Ignore everything else and don't come back without it." He waited for Parson to acknowledge his instructions then hung up. A nasty smile cracked his face. He turned his computer off and walked to a large bookcase. Withdrawing an ancient text he'd found in a market-place in Cairo, he began reading about the golden globe of goodness.

# SEVEN

Behind the closed and booby-trapped door of their bedroom Mitchell and Bradley were making plans for revenge. Mitchell rubbed his leg. It was still sore. He opened his toy chest and took out some itching powder and several stink bombs. Once armed, Mitchell rummaged deeper into the chest until he found several pots of coloured face paint. He smeared a line of black paint diagonally across his face then added green until his face resembled a military camouflage mask. When he was happy with the result, he passed the pot to his brother. He watched as Bradley dipped a pudgy digit in the paint and drew a cross down the bridge of his nose and through his eyebrows, then he began splurging the paint on in a random fashion. The result was less like a jungle commando and more like a clown who got caught in a rainstorm and his make-up had run.

Mitchell waited until Bradley had finished, then passed him a balloon filled with itching powder. Mitchell was armed with a high-powered water gun containing a nasty combination of foul-smelling grease and oil.

"How come you get the coolest weapon?" Bradley complained.

Mitchell shrugged. "I'm oldest."

Bradley grunted unhappily. It sucked being the youngest.

Mitchell gave Bradley a military-style hand signal indicating they should "move out". Bradley punched the air in excitement. It was going to be a fun night.

The two brothers crept down the hall, stopping outside Sophie's room as planned. Mitchell placed his hand on the door and was just about to burst inside when he heard strange sounds coming from his grandmother's room. He made a snap decision concluding that Sophie and Callum must be with Gran. Perfect, he thought. We can get them all at once.

He waved Bradley away from the door then the two of them moved along the hallway. They burst into Rose's room, whooping as they entered.

It took a few seconds for Mitchell's eyes to adjust to the gloom. A purple haze hung from the ceiling and Mitchell felt like he was looking through a watery glass of Ribena. He stepped back in shock as two large faceless shapes turned towards him. The intruders had square, pig-like snouts and cold plastic-covered eyes that gleamed in the half-light. Mitchell didn't realize he was seeing humans wearing gas masks; all he knew was that one of the monsters was using a screeching machine to suck his gran's brain out of her ear.

Mitchell reacted in pure panic. He screamed and raised his water gun. He jerked the trigger and a thick jet of oil and grease squirted from the gun, spraying all over the intruders. He twisted to see his petrified brother follow his lead.

Bradley threw the itching-powder-filled balloon at the biggest monster. Then he sank to the floor, the dissipating mist still strong enough to do its job. Mitchell kicked his brother's body aside and made for the door. Before he'd gone two steps the mist overwhelmed him and he joined Bradley on the carpet.

In the bedroom next door, Callum and Sophie were busily preparing for the night ahead when they heard Mitchell's and Bradley's war cries.

Callum was puzzled. "What's going on?"

Sophie shrugged. "No idea. The boys aren't stupid enough to attack Rose, are they?"

Callum wasn't sure. "They're pretty dumb. We'd better check it out."

The two friends put on their nose plugs, grabbed their kits and left the room.

The purple mist leaking from the open door to Rose's room had thinned considerably, its sleep-inducing effects also fading.

Callum and Sophie moved cautiously into the room. The first thing they saw were Mitchell's and Bradley's bodies unconscious on the floor.

Then they noticed a huge man standing guard at the foot of Rose's bed and another man with dreadlocks holding what looked like a shrunken vacuum cleaner against her head. They watched in shock as the dreadlocked man fought for control of the machine, which screamed like a horror movie actress. Flames leaped from the engine.

Callum had no idea what the men were doing to his gran, but he knew it wasn't good. He could see Rose's head convulsing and her eyeballs were beginning to bulge. A hot rage filled him. He gripped the push rims on his chair and surged forwards, but the wheels caught on Bradley's foot and he came to a sudden halt.

His voice cracked with anger. "Leave my gran alone."

The man with the vacuum cleaner looked up at the sound of Callum's voice, but before he could reply, the goodness contained in Rose's brain was finally wrenched from her skull and was sucked into the Perspex Thermos with a wet *thwock*. It shone like a miniature golden beacon. The force of the extraction threw the man backwards, and he landed in a heap on the bedroom floor, the Thermos containing the golden goodness clasped against his chest.

The thug reacted with speed, removing the suction cup and tube then replacing it with a screw-top lid, effectively trapping the goodness in a Perspex prison.

With the brain sucker removed, Rose flopped back on the bed. For a few seconds her body jerked like a fish stranded out of water, then she fell into a heavy sleep.

Callum reversed, freeing his chair from Bradley's foot, then sped towards the man with dreadlocks. "Whatever you took from my gran, you'd better give it back," he snarled.

The larger thug stepped in front of him, blocking his way. He lifted his gas mask and spoke. His voice was deep and threatening. "Back off, kid. This don't concern you."

Callum stayed put. He shouted to Sophie without taking his eyes off the big man. "Call the police."

Sophie moved swiftly. She raced out of the room, searching for a phone.

The man with dreadlocks pulled himself off the floor. He packed the vacuum cleaner and Thermos in a platinum briefcase, removed his mask and joined the other thug in front of Callum. He looked the boy straight in the eye. "Move."

"Not until you give me that." Callum pointed to the case in his hand.

The man shook his head. "It ain't gonna happen." He nudged his partner impatiently. "We don't have time for this – let's go."

Stepping forwards, the huge man reached for Callum's wheelchair. Callum unclipped the torch Sophie had given him and pressed the second button. The metal rod shot out the end and clicked into place. He raised the torch above his head threateningly. "Touch my chair and you'll be sorry."

The thug snorted. "You wouldn't dare." He reached out with a ham-sized hand and grabbed the side of the Thunderkit.

Callum struck without hesitation. The metal rod hissed through the air and smashed into the knuckles on the man's left hand. Howling in pain, the thug pulled back his damaged appendage.

Callum held firm in the doorway. "I warned you."

The dreadlocked man pushed past his injured partner, his eyes narrowed. He reached into his belt and withdrew a compact Glock 19 pistol and pointed it at Callum. "We're not playing games here, kid. Put that device down."

Callum didn't move.

The man cocked the weapon. "Your choice, boy."

Sophie rushed back into the room. She saw the gun pointed at her friend and stopped dead. "He's not kidding, Cal."

For a few heart-stopping seconds Callum was still then he retracted the rod, placed the torch back in its pouch and slowly rolled his wheelchair out of the way.

The two intruders pushed past and ran out the bedroom door.

Sophie kneeled beside Callum. She was breathing fast and her voice was shaky. "I called the police. They are on their way."

"Get a trace on them; we need to know where they're going." Callum handed her his weapons kit.

Sophie hesitated and looked towards Rose. "Is your gran OK?"

Callum rolled over to the bed and placed a hand on her pale forehead, then stroked her grey hair. He looked back to Sophie. "I don't know. I'll stay with her until the police get here. You go, but be careful."

Sophie followed the retreating thieves. She made it outside in time to see the men running towards a black van parked directly across the road. She sprinted behind a large tree, pulled out the dart gun and cocked it. The ball of gum containing the tracer fell in front of the gas-fired spring that would launch it from the barrel. Sophie aimed at the men, said a silent prayer and fired.

The gum bullet sped across the road and hit the end of the briefcase that the dreadlocked man carried. It stuck fast.

She watched as he threw the case into the back of the vehicle then leaped inside. The wheels of the van spun and the vehicle roared off into the night.

Sophie had fired just in time.

# EIGHT

Darryl drove with his window down. It was a doomed attempt to keep the stink that covered his clothes from filling the car. Beside him, Parson fidgeted in the seat, scratching himself and rubbing his back against the upholstery.

Darryl's hands were a mess. The knuckles on his left hand were the size and colour of ducks' eggs where the torch had struck them, and his broken finger throbbed painfully. But even the henchmen's obvious discomfort couldn't dampen their spirits. Darryl gave Parson a grin. "The boss'll be happy."

"Yeah, we've come through big-time. He'll

probably give us a huge promotion."

"You reckon?"

"Definitely. We got golden goodness. Even the boss ain't done that."

"What about those kids? They saw us."

Parson's lips thinned. "We probably shouldn't mention that. You know what he's like about keeping a low profile."

Darryl scooped a handful of slime off the front of his overalls and threw it out the window. He pointed to the grease on both their overalls. "How do we explain all this then?"

"We say we fell in a ditch." Parson frantically scratched at his neck.

"That don't make us sound very professional."

"True. OK, if he asks, I'll think of somethin', but we don't tell him about the kids."

Darryl frowned again. He blew on his swollen knuckles. Stupid kids. They were putting a dampener on the henchmen's moment of triumph.

Parson was thinking the same thing. "I should have shot 'em," he said.

Darryl nodded. "Yeah, next time, eh?"

The aftermath of the intrusion at 11 Success Court was intense. Ken and Rebecca had woken from the gas just after Mitchell and Bradley came around. The boys were terrified by what they had seen and had locked themselves in their room. Ken and Rebecca were convinced they'd been attacked by aliens and had called almost every branch of the emergency services. They rushed about issuing instructions to police and ambulance crews and requesting round-the-clock protection. Several firemen loitered outside the house, looking for either a fire or a cat stuck up a tree. The family cat, however, hadn't moved from her spot at the bottom of the stairs. She was the only one to remain calm; compared to what she put up with from Mitchell and Bradley on a daily basis, this was a walk in the park.

Callum wasn't really aware of the chaos that surrounded him. He sat next to Rose's bed, watching anxiously as a male paramedic examined his grandmother. Sophie stood beside the bedroom window. Lights from the ambulance and police cars that were parked in the driveway played over her face – red then blue, red then blue. She also watched the paramedic work.

The man wrapped a blood pressure cuff around Rose's thin arm, pumped it up and placed the end of a stethoscope under the cuff. Rose made an irritated tutting sound with her tongue. She'd been in a foul mood since being woken and could remember nothing of her midnight assault. She grabbed the end of the stethoscope and spoke directly into it. Her tone was uncharacteristically sharp.

"I've already told you there's nothing wrong with me, you moron. Take this thing off my arm and go away."

The paramedic wrenched his stethoscope from his ears and struggled to maintain a professional demeanour. "If you'll just be patient for a little longer, madam, I've nearly finished. I just need to check you for concussion."

The paramedic took out a torch and switched it on. He shone the light in Rose's left eye. The old lady slapped his arm away.

"Shine that thing in my face again, sonny boy, and it won't be me that's concussed," she snapped.

Callum tried to calm his grandmother down. "He only wants to help, Gran."

"I don't need help, and I don't need to be poked and prodded by weak-brained fools. Get out of here. All of you."

With that she turned her back on them and pulled the blankets over her head.

The paramedic shrugged, packed up his gear and headed out of the room. Callum followed him to the door. He lowered his voice. "I'm sorry about that. She's normally very sweet. Could her injury be causing her to act like this?"

The man snorted. "I doubt it. Apart from being extremely rude, there's nothing wrong with her."

After the paramedic had left, Callum pulled Sophie into the hallway. "That was weird. He just did a basic check. I thought they'd admit her to hospital at the very least."

Sophie frowned. "Me too. Especially since she's acting so strangely."

As they spoke, a policeman walked into the

hall. He was a big man in his late thirties with grumpy eyes and a big nose, under which perched a large bushy moustache. It looked like a moth had crash-landed into his face.

He spoke in a booming voice. "I take it you are the children who witnessed the alleged incident?"

Callum nodded. He didn't like the way the policeman had stressed the word "alleged".

"I'm Sergeant Oliver Bright of the Inner City Police Division. Please tell me exactly what you saw."

Callum wasted no time relating the evening's events, with Sophie adding any details he omitted. When he finished speaking, the policeman stared at him for a few seconds and then said, "Hmmm." Callum had the distinct impression he didn't believe a word they were telling him.

The policeman motioned for Callum and Sophie to go back into Rose's room. "I suppose I'd better speak to the alleged victim then." That word again.

As the policeman strode over to Rose, Callum offered a warning. "My grandmother's very tired and might be a bit, um, difficult."

Sergeant Bright snorted, causing his moustache to wobble. "Son, I deal with hardened criminals every day. I think I can handle an elderly lady."

He shook the blankets where Rose's shoulder was hidden. "Excuse me, madam," he said loudly. "It's the police. I'd like a quick word."

A muffled voice came from under the blankets. "I don't care if it's the king of the world. I'm sleeping; go away."

Sergeant Bright carried on undeterred. "You are speaking to me, so clearly you are not sleeping. Please remove the blanket from your head and answer my questions."

Rose tossed the blankets off and sat upright, her eyes blazing with indignation. She stared long and hard at the policeman. "Actually, I have some questions to ask you. Why is a delicate, law-abiding senior citizen such as me being harassed by a constant flow of dim-witted people? And why do you have such a ridiculously unfashionable moustache? It makes you look like a walrus in a uniform."

Callum winced and looked at Sophie, whose mouth hung open in shock.

"Madam, please," spluttered the policeman. "There's no need for such unpleasant and personal ab—"

Rose cut him off. "Oh for heaven's sake, get on with your questions before you start blubbering."

Sergeant Bright was clearly shaken. He was not used to being spoken to in such a manner. "According to witnesses…" He took time to compose himself by referring to his notebook and glancing at Callum and Sophie. They shuffled nervously. "…you were the victim of a serious assault tonight. Can you please tell me about this incident?"

Rose sighed. "I'll tell you this once, and I'll speak slowly so my words won't be too much for your minuscule brain. As far as I can remember, there was no 'incident'. Obviously, the children have had some sort of nightmare and you people have completely overreacted. I'd have thought you'd have better things to do than poke your sizeable nose and big, flat feet into other people's business."

A wounded look passed over Sergeant Bright's face. Callum felt sorry for him.

The policeman drew himself up to full height. "I'll have you know, madam, that I have surprisingly dainty feet for a man of my size." He then tucked his notebook back into a pocket in his uniform and left the room. As he went, Rose flipped over, muttering under her breath. Callum thought she said "Go boil your head" but couldn't be sure.

Half an hour after the police and ambulance crew left, Callum wheeled quietly over to Sophie's room. He gave a soft rap on the door. Sophie opened it and let him in. She sat on the bed. "Well, that sucked."

Callum agreed. "The police didn't believe a word we said."

"Mitchell and Bradley blathering on about space monsters isn't exactly helping our case," said Sophie with a sigh. "And your gran can't remember a thing." She pouted. "Besides, what do we know? We're just kids."

"We know what we saw," Callum said, determination in his eyes. "I don't care what the police say – those thugs sucked something out of Gran and we're going to get it back."

Sophie flopped onto her stomach and cupped her head in her hands. "What do you think they took?"

Callum scratched his jaw. He looked tired. "I don't know. She's acting very strange though. She was incredibly rude to the paramedic and the policeman. I've never seen her like that, and she didn't even ask us for our side of the story, which is not like her either."

"Have you talked to your aunt about it?"

Callum nodded. "I tried, but she completely dismissed me. She said that Rose was just getting grumpy in her old age then told me to go to bed." He sighed. "We've got to find those burglars. Any luck with the tracker?"

Sophie pulled an iPhone from under her pillow. She entered the map application and the word "Scan" popped up. Sophie had made a few adjustments to the phone, completely voiding the manufacturer's guarantee. She touched the screen and waited as a series of street maps near their current location scrolled up. After a minute the words "Nil result" flashed. Sophie shook her head. "They must be out of range."

"We'll try again tomorrow. I'd better go. If we're caught talking, Rebecca will have a major meltdown." Callum rolled to the door.

Sophie held his gaze. "It'll be all right, Cal. We'll fix this."

"I really hope so, Soph. Rose is all the family I have, or at least the only family I actually like."

He left the room before his best friend could see how upset he really was.

No one got up early the following morning. When Ken and Rebecca did rise, they were really grumpy. Rebecca clattered about in the kitchen, making a rather poor breakfast for her guests, and Ken went straight into his home office without saying a word and shut the door.

Mitchell and Bradley were a different story. They were subdued, regarding Callum and Sophie with a mixture of fear and awe. Mitchell approached Callum in the bathroom as he washed his hands before breakfast. He peeped around the door keeping his distance. His brother stood behind him in the hallway. Mitchell spoke quietly.

"You guys saw the monsters last night, didn't you?"

Callum nodded. "They weren't monsters; they were men in gas masks."

"What did they want?"

"We don't know yet, but we're going to find out."

Bradley popped out from behind his brother. "We got 'em you know."

Callum raised an eyebrow and waited for Bradley to continue.

"We sprayed 'em with grease and smashed 'em with itching powder."

Callum laughed. "I suppose that had been meant for us."

"No," lied Mitchell.

"Yes," said Bradley.

"Yes," Mitchell finally admitted. "But we're not out to get you any more, not if you chased the monsters out of our house."

"Truce then?" Callum extended his hand.

Mitchell spat into his palm. "Truce."

Callum hesitated then spat as well. They shook hands. Callum could feel Mitchell's spit squelching against his palm. He tried very hard not to shudder with revulsion.

When the brothers had left, Callum washed his hands again, thoroughly.

Sophie helped Callum wheel backwards up the stairs so he could check on his grandmother. It was unusual for Callum to be up before his gran. She normally rose at seven sharp, bustling around, preparing herself and the household for the day. But it was nine o'clock and she still hadn't stirred. She just lay on her back, snoring. This was also peculiar. Callum had never known Rose to snore before. This morning she sounded like a hippopotamus with a head cold.

After watching his grandmother rasp unglamorously for a few minutes, Callum decided to act. He wheeled over to her bed and gently nudged the mattress with his hand.

Rose gave a final snort then one of her eyes

fluttered open. She stared at Callum.

"What do you want?" she grunted.

Callum was taken aback. There was no cheery "Good morning" or a pleasant "How did you sleep?"

"Um, breakfast's ready, Gran. Everyone's in the kitchen."

Rose kept only one eye open.

"Not hungry," she said and rolled onto her side, away from her grandson.

Callum gently nudged the bed again. "Are you all right, Gran?"

"I was happily asleep until you started banging about like an elephant with a bee up its trunk," snapped Rose. "Suppose I'd better get up now. Get me a cup of tea."

Callum rushed out of the room, stunned. He'd assumed that his grandmother's rudeness from the previous night had been caused by shock, but she hadn't improved. As Callum made tea, he thought about her behaviour and knew instantly what was wrong. He made sure that his aunt and uncle weren't within earshot then called Sophie into the kitchen.

"I've worked out what those men took from Gran," he whispered.

Sophie moved closer. "What?"

Callum placed the teacup on a saucer, handing it to Sophie to carry. "Follow me, you'll see."

Moments later Callum and Sophie were outside Rose's bedroom door. Callum tapped lightly on the woodwork. Rose's voice came from within. "Who is it?"

"It's Callum with your tea."

"About bloody time. Come in then."

Callum and Sophie looked at each other before entering the room. Rose was still in bed but was sitting up, pillows propped behind her. Her nightgown was rumpled and creased, and her hair was a mess. She'd made no effort to tidy herself up.

"Good morning, Mrs McCullock," said Sophie, cheerfully.

"Mummmph," replied Rose. "Where's my tea?"

Sophie handed Rose the cup and saucer. She snatched it from the girl's hand, gave another grunt then poured some tea out of the cup into the saucer. Tipping the saucer to her lips, she drank the tea with one long, noisy slurp.

Callum and Sophie couldn't believe their eyes; Rose normally drank in delicate sips with her pinkie extended.

Once she had finished slurping, Rose wiped her nose on the sleeve of her nightgown and let out an almighty belch.

Callum's jaw dropped.

"What are you two staring at?" demanded Rose.

"Nothing, Gran." Callum grabbed Sophie by the arm and led her to the door. "We'll leave you in peace."

The two friends left the room to the sound of Rose breaking wind. Sophie's eyes were wide with astonishment.

"That was incredible. She was rude and crass and…" Sophie searched for the right word, "…well, horrible."

Callum nodded. "There's no doubt about it. Those men have taken Gran's manners and grace and generosity and pleasantness, and everything that makes her such a kind, loving person. It's like they've sucked the goodness right out of her."

"You're right." Sophie gasped. "Why would anyone want to do that?"

"I don't know," said Callum, grimly. "But we've got to find out who did it and get her back to normal. And we've got two days to do it."

Sophie was puzzled. "Two days?"

"In two days' time Gran has her final interview with the welfare officer, and if they see her like this, they'll take me away from her, Thanxton and all my friends, and place me with Rebecca's family." Callum's voice shook with emotion; he was close to tears.

Sophie was in real danger of losing her best friend. She touched his arm. "Don't worry, Cal. We'll get your gran back to how she was before; I promise."

Callum fought for composure. "We have to. We just have to."

# NINE

Lester was ecstatic when his employees returned with the golden globe of goodness. As soon as Darryl and Parson arrived back in his warehouse lair, he ran over to the van. He tore the briefcase from Parson's hands and pulled out the tube, barely glancing at the men. Lester had eyes for only one thing. He scrutinized the golden glowing mass inside the tube. Clasping it to his chest, he smiled slow and long.

Lester carefully placed the cylinder on a nearby workbench and switched his attention to his henchmen. The first thing he noticed was the stink. They smelled as if they'd been swimming in a sewer. Darryl was particularly ripe and streaks of thick grease covered his overalls. Parson constantly scratched at a white powder that dusted his head and chest.

For a few moments Lester said nothing. Darryl and Parson shuffled uneasily. Finally, Lester spoke. "You did well tonight, exceeded expectations."

Darryl smiled.

"Don't get smug – expectations were low."

Darryl stopped smiling.

"However, you have brought me something of great value and shall be rewarded. You are both promoted from henchmen to right-hand men."

Lester moved closer to Darryl and dipped a finger in a patch of grease. He held the blackened finger before Darryl's face. "Clearly, this mission was not without its trials. Got anything to tell me?"

Darryl looked at his feet and said nothing.

Turning to Parson, Lester ran a different finger through the white powder on his chest, sniffed it then tasted it with the tip of his tongue. "Itching powder, if I'm not mistaken." Lester rounded on his henchmen. "I hope you haven't been seen by any children," he roared.

Parson shook his head so hard it nearly fell off. "No, Boss, definitely not. One of the brats had booby trapped his room, and we walked into it, but they didn't see us. No way."

Darryl hurriedly joined in. "All the kids were knocked out by the gas, Boss, comatose. I'm pretty certain we weren't seen."

"Pretty certain?" Lester circled them like a shark.

Darryl corrected himself. "Absolutely certain, Boss. We weren't seen. Like ghosts, we were."

Lester drew a curved knife from his belt. Parson and Darryl stiffened in fear. Lester used the knife to sharpen his talon-like nails. He smiled. "That's fine then. I'm pleased you weren't seen. Secrecy is very important to me; it allows this little operation to remain undetected. So if you had been spotted, I'd be very upset. OK, you can go now. I imagine you'd like a shower."

Darryl's and Parson's bodies sagged with relief. They prepared to leave.

"One more thing," said Lester. "If I find out you've been lying, I will kill you – slowly and painfully."

He picked up the cylinder containing the golden globe and left the garage without another word.

Callum and Sophie climbed into the rear of Rose's car with a huge sense of relief. It was just after twelve o'clock and the atmosphere in the house had been arctic all morning.

Ken had remained in his office, only coming out to say a curt goodbye. Rebecca clumped around the house with all the grace and charm of a wounded gorilla. Rose stayed entrenched in her room, as did Mitchell and Bradley. Callum and Sophie felt about as welcome as a zit on the night of the school ball.

Callum watched from the car as his grand-mother said goodbye to Rebecca. It was distressing to see his normally well-groomed gran in such a state. Her hair was uncombed, her make-up looked like it had been applied with a spray gun and her clothing was mismatched and crumpled. Her mood hadn't improved either. Callum wound down the car window so he could hear what she was saying. Rose's voice was loud and brash.

"...bed was lumpy and you look like you need a decent meal; you're too thin and too stupid for your own good. As for your worthless husband, I've seen puddles of mud with more spine. You won't see me back in a hurry."

Rose turned her back on her stunned daughter and stomped towards the car. Before getting in, she added one final thing. "I must say though, I quite like the boys."

Callum whispered to Sophie, horrified. "Did you hear that?"

"That confirms our theory," said Sophie. "No one with any goodness left could like those kids."

Rose got in the car and slammed the door. "What are you brats jabbering about?"

"Nothing, Gran," Callum replied quickly.

"You'd better keep the noise down. I've got a headache and don't need you two yapping in the back."

Rose started the car and drove away without waving goodbye. Callum and Sophie sat in the rear, afraid to talk. As they headed out of the suburbs, Sophie typed a note on her phone and passed it to Callum. It read "Tracker activated".

This was their only hope of finding the thieves.

Sophie clicked a button on her phone bringing up an unauthorised screen she had downloaded from the Internet. She plugged in her headphones and passed one of the earpieces to Callum. If Rose checked on them, it would look like they were sitting quietly, listening to music.

Just before they left the city limits, the phone's screen came alive and a pulsating red dot appeared on the map. Sophie gave Callum an excited nudge. The signal was only two streets from their current location. It was time to initiate the plan they had come up with before leaving his cousins' house. Callum pulled the headphone from his ear and leaned over the seat to speak to his grandmother. He pointed to a roadside café.

"Can we stop for lunch please, Gran?"

The old lady glanced at her wristwatch. It was

12.30. She made an annoyed clicking sound with her tongue and grudgingly swung the car into the café's car park.

"You're lucky I'm hungry."

Sophie waited until Rose was at the counter ordering a second helping of cake then slipped a sedative she'd borrowed from Rebecca's bathroom cabinet into the old lady's tea. Callum knew even Bad Rose wouldn't let them go wandering around the industrial estate by themselves. Their only option was to ensure that she had a nice long nap. Once Callum's grandmother showed signs of drowsiness, they helped her back to the car and installed her in the driver's seat with a pillow behind her head. Before long Rose fell into a deep slumber and the sound of a congested hippopotamus could be heard again.

Ten minutes and fifty-two locator blips later Sophie and Callum were in front of Big Al's Used Car Parts, the business that hid Lester's lair. At first sight the business seemed to be just an auto parts yard. Customers filed in and out of a roomy retail shop that sold everything from chrome wheel nuts to those air pumps that make a *pssspt* sound. Several shop assistants in Big Al's uniforms milled around the customers, helping them to buy things their cars didn't really need.

"Are you sure this is the place?" said Callum.

Sophie examined the locator screen. The signal was definitely coming from somewhere within the building. She nodded.

Callum jumped a gutter and rolled his wheelchair onto a concrete driveway leading to the rear of the building. "Let's find it then."

They rounded the corner and stopped dead. Directly in front of them was a sentry box controlling traffic in and out of the rear of the warehouse.

A barrier arm extended across the concrete, blocking the way. A large man dressed in a black uniform and wearing dark sunglasses sat in the box. The security guard turned his head to face Callum and Sophie. He watched them very closely from behind his glasses. There was a loud rumble and a freight train blasted past not far from the end of the warehouse. The security guard didn't react.

He kept an unwavering eye on Callum and Sophie.

"No way through there," Sophie said out the corner of her mouth.

Callum agreed. "Let's see what the other side of the building's like."

He swung his wheelchair around and headed back along the footpath in front of the store. Sophie followed. As she walked, she noticed there were security cameras mounted on the roof at each corner of the warehouse. She caught up to Callum and nodded towards the cameras. He gave her a quizzical look.

"Top of the line," she whispered.

The other side of the building contained a few car spaces and a series of drains diverting what sounded like a considerable flow of water away from the industrial complex. Seagulls circled in the distance, and Callum guessed they were close to the ocean. Beyond the car park was a patch of broken ground and a long grassed area. A solid chain-metal fence surrounded the grass. Tight circles of barbed wire topped the fence. The barrier followed the rear two thirds of the warehouse then disappeared around the back of the building.

Callum could see an open doorway just inside the fence. It led into the rear of the warehouse. He rolled to the end of the car park and surveyed the broken ground. It was littered with rubble, including broken bricks and offcuts of concrete. Even with the wheelchair in out mode it would be difficult to get across.

"I'll have a look," offered Sophie. Callum nodded reluctantly. He hated not being able to do it himself.

Sophie stepped across the rubble and walked up to the fence. She made sure no one was watching then took hold of the wire and gave it a gentle shake. Sophie called back to Callum.

"I think I could cut through—"

She got no further. A large snarling German shepherd dog burst from the doorway and leaped at her, its jaws snapping as it lunged. Sophie jumped backwards, removing her hand from the fence milliseconds before the dog hit the wire. If Sophie had been a fraction slower, the dog would have taken off her fingers.

The dog barked frantically, and Sophie scampered back to Callum.

"P-pretty heavy security for a car parts yard," she stammered.

"Yeah, something's not right here." He watched her for a second. She was visibly shaken. "You OK?"

"Gave me a fright, that's all."

The dog's barking subsided to a low growl.

"We'd better get out of here."

Callum and Sophie retreated to the front of the building. Sophie sat on a low wall in the car park, taking a moment to calm her nerves. Callum pulled up beside her. "That bug of yours has audio, doesn't it?"

"Yeah, if we're close enough, we might hear something. Good thinking."

Sophie pulled out her phone, plugged in her headphones and passed an earpiece to Callum. A low hiss buzzed in Callum's ear, then to his surprise a man's voice cut through. Sophie and Callum looked at each other in astonishment as the voice went on, crackly but clearly audible.

"Newly acquired golden globe of goodness may be the breakthrough I've been looking for. It's very rare and is found only in an ambassador of goodness – a person, usually a teacher, who passes their goodness on to others. The globe contains the ability to bypass the defensive field of ordinary blobs of goodness, normally for teaching purposes. If I can run the energy bolt through the golden globe, penetration and destruction of regular blobs of goodness may be possible."

Sophie and Callum exchanged an alarmed look.

"The golden globe he's talking about must be Gran's," whispered Callum.

"And he wants to destroy everyone's goodness!"

Callum shrugged and held his finger to his lips. Sophie fell quiet. They both wanted to hear more.

# TEN

Lester paced excitedly around his laboratory, Dictaphone in his hand. Ancient texts lay open on his desk and his computer showed an internet page entitled "Weapons Modification". The aluminium briefcase with Sophie's tracer bug still attached (and unfortunately for Lester, unnoticed) sat in a corner of the room.

Another torpedo tube containing a freshly caught green blob of goodness dangled from the robotic arm at one end of the bench. A similarly shaped cylinder housing Rose's golden globe sat in a moulded foam rubber box on the floor. Lester placed the Dictaphone on the bench, carefully removed the cylinder containing the golden globe and walked to the opposite end of the bench. He picked up his energy weapon and clicked the cylinder into a modified chamber in the body of the weapon. The energy bolt would now pass directly through the golden globe as it discharged. He plugged in the weapon and restarted his Dictaphone.

"Golden globe weapons test number one. Minimal power."

Lester aimed the weapon at the green blob of goodness and fired. The blue energy bolt that shot from the barrel was now tinged with gold, and it passed through the tube and struck the blob with a fizzing crack. This time the tube remained undamaged, and the bolt met no resistance as it slammed into the body of the blob. With an animal-like shriek, the blob blackened then disintegrated, leaving behind nothing more than a wisp of smoke and a small pile of ash.

At 16 Hamstead Street on the other side of the city, Caine Wentworth sat bolt upright on the couch he'd been lounging on. He had a sudden desire to throw a rock through the neighbour's window and then blame it on his brother. And with this thought came absolutely no guilt, conscience or morality at all. It was as if every last trace of goodness had been obliterated from his brain.

Lester let out a whoop of victory. He gabbled excitedly into his Dictaphone.

"Success! Tube undamaged, goodness completely destroyed." He examined the cylinder containing the golden globe. "Limited wastage of globe detected, but nothing significant."

He paced the room, his brain churning. He continued to dictate. "By combining the golden globe with a massive energy blast, I should be able to send out a pulse that will destroy the goodness of every person in the country, perhaps even the world. Beginning construction of the bad bomb."

Lester turned off his dictaphone and picked up his tools.


Callum removed his earpiece and motioned for Sophie to do the same. Her eyes were wide.

"A bad bomb. I don't like the sound of that."

Callum shook his head. "The guy's a psycho. If he sets off his bomb, he'll probably destroy Gran's goodness for ever and make everyone in the world like Mitchell and Bradley. Can you imagine what that'd be like?"

Sophie shuddered. "We can't let that happen. Should we call the police?"

"Yes, this is too big for us to handle by ourselves. We should probably talk to Sergeant Bright; maybe now he'll realize what's happened to Gran. Use your mobile and we can direct them to the warehouse."

Sophie took out her phone and called the city's main police station. She activated the phone's speaker so Callum could hear the conversation and waited. The call was answered within a few rings.

"Central Police," said an unfriendly female voice.

Sophie remained polite. "Sergeant Bright please."

The call was transferred and several minutes later Sophie had related their story to the sergeant.

His reaction was not what they had hoped for.

"A globe of golden goodness and a bad bomb!" he spluttered. "That's ridiculous. What proof do you have?"

Sophie patiently explained that they'd over-heard everything through a bug she had planted on the goodness thieves. This was too much for Sergeant Bright.

"You kids have been watching too many James Bond movies. Even if I wanted to get a warrant to search this warehouse, which I don't, any judge would throw me out on my ear. Goodness thieves! Preposterous! Now go away before I lock you up for wasting police time." The line went dead.

"That went well," said Sophie.

Callum clenched his fists in frustration. "Typical. Just like what happened at my aunt's house. Adults never listen to kids. We've got no option now; we're going to have to sort this out ourselves."

"OK, so how do we do that?"

Callum thought hard. "The first thing we need to do is get Gran's goodness back. He can't make his bomb without that. Then we'll find some hard evidence to take to the police, something so convincing they'll have to believe us."

Callum studied the warehouse.

"I think we should come back later, when it's dark and the security guard has gone home. I'm not sure how we'll get back here though. We can hardly ask Gran for a lift."

Sophie thought for a minute then smiled. "Don't worry. I've got an idea."

"What is it?"

"Wait and see. It'll take me most of tomorrow to prepare. I've got some engineering to do."

Callum didn't like being kept in the dark but knew better than to press Sophie. She'd tell him when she was ready.

Rose was still fast asleep when they returned to the car. Callum gently nudged her. She snapped awake. "What? Who? Where are we?"

"We're about to leave the city, Gran, on our way home. You just had a nap."

She wiped a line of drool from her mouth with her hand.

"Pity," she said as she opened the car window and flicked the string of drool out onto the street. "The city's growing on me."

The remainder of the trip back to Thanxton was chaotic. The new Bad Rose was a rude and aggressive driver. She was constantly trying to pass other vehicles and leaned on the horn if motorists didn't get out of her way. Callum spent most of the journey with his arms braced against the seat in front of him and his eyes closed. Even Sophie, who liked going fast, was looking distinctly nervous.

They arrived home in record time, and as Sophie hopped gratefully from the car she noticed steam coming from under the bonnet. She was pointing it out to Callum when Rose announced she was feeling unwell and disappeared into the house.

Callum watched his grandmother leave with a mixture of fear and concern. "I can't believe this has changed her so much."

Sophie approached his wheelchair. A tape measure appeared in her hands and she stretched it between the front wheels.

"It's not surprising really. She's been sweet and

good all her life; having that ripped away must have altered her entire personality. Try and remember that underneath she's still your gran."

"I'll try, but it's not going to be easy. She's becoming more offensive with every passing minute. She wants me to get some sardines out of her false teeth when I go inside." Callum shuddered.

Sophie stretched the tape measure along the side of the wheelchair. "Don't worry. By the end of tomorrow night we'll have her back to normal and will probably have saved the world as well. I wonder if we'll get a medal."

"That would be cool." Callum watched as she reached under his wheelchair and measured its width. "What are you doing?"

Sophie stood up and wiped dust from her trouser legs. "All will be revealed later," she said, much to Callum's annoyance. Sophie went back to the car, grabbed her sports bag from the boot and slung it over her shoulder. "Come by tomorrow afternoon – everything should be ready then." She gave Callum a mysterious smile and headed home.

Callum watched her walk away, deep in

thought. He stayed outside long after Sophie had gone. He was in no hurry to spend the evening with Rose.

The first day back at school after the break held one unexpected event. Jinx's maths classroom blew up. Having one of Jinx's classrooms explode wasn't particularly unusual. So far this year he'd reduced the science and English rooms to rubble. Geography class had been flooded and history had fallen into a previously undiscovered underground cavern. Up to this point, however, mathematics had remained safe. It wasn't a big explosion and no one was hurt, but it did liven up an otherwise dull day.

Callum caught up with Jinx at lunchtime. The red-headed boy was sitting by himself under a tree near the ruined wall of his classroom. He looked up as Callum approached and kicked his shoe into the ground.

He nodded glumly towards the debris. "I suppose I'll get the blame for that. Even though it was a ruptured gas main that did the damage."

Callum stopped next to him. "I heard the gas line broke right under your desk."

"Yeah, just as I dropped my compass. It hit the leg of my chair and caused a spark. Next second … *BOOM* … half the wall's gone. Just my luck."

"Don't worry about it. Everyone knows don't do stuff like that on purpose. Anyway, I've got something really important to tell you, so listen carefully."

Jinx's eyes widened as the story progressed.

"No way," he said, and "You're kidding" and "That's insane" and "Wish I'd been there".

By the end of the story Jinx was incensed. "He stole goodness from your gran and wants to destroy everyone else's! That sucks. So, what are we going to do about it?"

"*We* aren't going to do anything. Soph and I are going to check out the warehouse tonight."

Jinx fixed his friend with a determined stare. "I'm going with you."

"There's no need. I've got it under control."

"Don't you want me to come?" A pained look crossed Jinx's face. "I thought we were friends."

"Of course we're friends. It might be quite dangerous, that's all, and I wouldn't ask you to put yourself at risk."

Jinx burst out laughing. "Getting up in the morning is risky for me. Come on, Cal. No one ever lets me do anything, and I really want to help. Please."

"OK, but you can't tell anyone," said Callum with a sigh. "I'll call you later and let you know what time we're leaving."

Jinx clapped him on the shoulder. "Brilliant. You won't regret this."

Callum hoped not. Then he realized he hadn't laid eyes on Sophie, which was odd as they shared several classes. He asked one of his teachers where she was and discovered she was away sick. Callum was certain she wasn't ill, which meant she had spent all day working out how to get them to the warehouse.

He was both excited and nervous about what Sophie would come up with, so he hurried around to her place as soon as school ended. He knocked on the front door and Sophie's mum answered. She was a rotund woman who wore an expression of constant concern on her face. This was probably due to being Sophie's mother.

"She's in the workshop as usual," said Mrs Barnsworth. "Make sure she has the heating on. I don't want her cold getting any worse."

Callum nodded and headed out of the house. He was sure of two things: that Sophie didn't have a cold and that she would be completely and utterly convinced that whatever she had made would solve all their problems. He was right on both counts.

Callum barely made it through the door before Sophie raced over, grabbed his wheelchair and pulled him to the workbench. A large white bedsheet lay on top of whatever it was Sophie had been working on.

"About time you got here. I've been ready for ages."

"You seem remarkably upbeat for someone who has been struck down by a nasty head cold."

Sophie shrugged. "I'm extremely resilient. Now, first things first. I finished your birthday present."

She grabbed a padded metal armrest from the workbench and bolted it to the right-hand side of the Thunderkit on a swivel. "It's retractable. You can click it in place or release it and flick it behind the chair out of the way." Sophie demonstrated by releasing the arm and swinging it behind the chair. She then brought it back beside the wheel and locked it.

Callum wasn't sure how much use the armrest would be, but he appreciated the effort Sophie had gone to. "Cheers, Soph. That's gr—"

Sophie cut him short. "You haven't seen the best bit yet." She turned Callum's chair until he faced the rear of the workshop. "Right, now pull the lever."

Callum examined the armrest and saw a small trigger on the inside. He gave it a gentle tug.

Callum and the chair suddenly rocked back as a small hook shot from the front of the armrest and wrapped around a wooden beam at the end of the room. "What the hell!" he exclaimed.

Sophie could barely contain her excitement. "Miniature grappling hook with six metres of high-tensile wire. Pull the trigger again."

Callum did as he was told. The wire tightened and the armrest hummed. Callum could feel his chair being dragged towards the beam the grapple was hooked around. He laughed aloud. "Ha, you've put in a winch."

Sophie nodded happily. "Yep. I know what you're like; you're gonna get this chair into all sorts of tricky spots and now, at least, you can get yourself back out."

Callum continued using the winch until the grapple was within reach. He loosened it and pulled the trigger again. The hook retracted and the unit snapped back into place at the front of the armrest, virtually undetectable.

Callum wheeled back to Sophie at the workbench. He had a huge grin on his face. "You are a genius."

"You don't know the half of it. Have a look at this."

She removed the bedsheet from the bench with a flourish. A square metal trolley that was slightly bigger than the base of Callum's wheelchair lay underneath. Four iron wheels were attached to the trolley. The wheels had smooth concave grooves cut into their outer rim. A raised, padded platform had been attached to the inside of the trolley. Four clips hung from the corners of the platform.

"What do you think?"

Callum hesitated. "I'm not sure. What am I looking at?"

Sophie gave a huff of impatience. "It's obvious. Do you remember the railway lines that ran behind the warehouse?"

"Yeah."

"Well, I've designed this trolley to run on the tracks." Sophie tapped the raised platform attached to the trolley with her finger. "We just clip your wheelchair onto this platform, put a motor on the back of the trolley, and we've got an instant train."

Callum examined the trolley. "Where will you be?" A look of horror crossed his face. "You're not sitting on my knee."

Sophie rolled her eyes. "As if. I'm going to stand on the rear strut of the trolley and strap myself to your wheelchair."

"Is there enough room on the trolley for Jinx? He wants to come with us."

"Should be." Sophie tapped the rear strut with a spanner. "I'll just reinforce this bar and make another strap. It'll be good to have another pair of eyes along."

"That's what I thought. I told him he can be our lookout. He's bringing a phone and a pair of binoculars with him." Callum paused, studying the trolley. "One tiny detail. What if we meet a real train coming the other way? We'll be toast."

"I thought of that. I'll check the train schedules before we go so we can time our departure. But I've added a fail-safe device in case something does go wrong."

Callum gave Sophie a nervous look. "And what would that be?"

"I don't want to go into the technical details," said Sophie, answering a little too swiftly, "but trust me; we'll be fine."

Callum's suspicions grew. "I'll need more information than that."

"No, you won't. You get all weird and twitchy

every time I mention anything that may involve a teeny explosion."

"Yeah, I'm funny like that." Callum decided not to push the point. "Let's just hope we don't have to use it." He sighed. "It's not like there's much option. The welfare officer confirmed their appointment; they're going to be at our house at eight o'clock tomorrow morning before school. We have to get Gran's goodness back by then."

Sophie's expression hardened. "Then there's nothing else to discuss. We go tonight."

# ELEVEN

It was a calm and peaceful evening. The sky was clear and full of stars. A three-quarter moon bathed the Earth in a pale glow. Conditions were perfect for their night-time mission.

The railway lines ran through the woods behind Thanxton. There was no station in the town itself. A water treatment plant was also situated on the edge of the woods, and it was here that Sophie, Jinx and Callum met at exactly 10 p.m. Well, Sophie and Callum were there at exactly ten; Jinx arrived at twenty past. He was delayed when a suicidal hedgehog named Tim threw himself under Jinx's bike, puncturing the tyres. Jinx was inconvenienced but unhurt. Tim survived with minor bruising and then skulked away to throw himself off a cliff (which he missed).

Callum had told his grandmother he was staying at Sophie's place for the evening. He didn't like lying, but extreme situations called for extreme measures. Callum had expected some resistance from Rose, but she didn't blink an eye. His grandmother was watching a reality TV show and had the television turned up very loud – something she had never done in the past. So when he asked for permission, all he received was an unresponsive grunt.

Jinx's parents seemed almost relieved when he said he'd be staying at Sophie's place. Their only comment was to ask if the Barnsworths' house insurance was up to date.

It was harder for Sophie to get away as her parents were very suspicious about the sudden and miraculous disappearance of her cold. Sophie was undeterred and slipped out her bedroom window after her parents had gone to bed.

Both Callum and Sophie were dressed in black.

Callum wore tracksuit bottoms, a T-shirt and a light rain jacket. Sophie wore blue-black jeans, a T-shirt and a hoodie. The bulge of a tool belt showed around her waist. Jinx had elected to dress in camouflaged clothing. He'd even blacked out his face with what looked suspiciously like crayon.

Sophie stifled a laugh when she saw him. "We're not going to war."

Jinx bristled. "A lookout's job is to blend in with his surroundings."

Callum clapped Jinx on the shoulder. "Ignore her. I think you look awesome."

Sophie had suggested meeting at the water treatment plant for two reasons: firstly, because there was a road behind it that led across the railway lines, which meant easy access for Callum's wheelchair; and secondly, it was a comfortable downhill bike ride from Sophie's house. This was important because Sophie had to transport the railway trolley, engine and surveillance tools to the meeting point, and it was quite a load. She had achieved this by attaching a long trailer to her bike and piling everything on that. It had been slow, unsteady going, but she made it with no mishaps.

Callum took a black backpack from the trailer to lighten the load. It was unexpectedly heavy. He laid it across his knees. He pointed to her tool belt. "If you've brought a pack, why do you need a tool belt?"

Sophie gave a dismissive wave. "I keep smaller stuff in there. Snack food, wire clippers, smoke bomb, concussion ball – that kind of thing."

Callum raised his eyebrows. "What's a concussion ball?"

"A globe that sends out a shock wave when it goes off. Completely disorientates anyone in a ten-metre radius."

"Where'd you get that?"

"Made it."

This wasn't good news. Anything Sophie made was almost always unpredictable and unstable. Callum looked warily at the bag on his lap and gave it a tentative poke. "What's in here then?"

"Just some mission essentials. Nothing explosive."

"Oh, that's all right then," said Callum sarcastically. He called to Jinx. "Did you bring the phone and the binoculars?"

Jinx patted a pouch that was clipped to his belt. "Yep."

"Right," said Callum. "Let's go."

They travelled the rest of the short distance to the railway crossing in silence.

The trio stopped just before the crossing's lights and barrier arm, and pulled into a gravel area to unload the trailer.

"Are you absolutely sure you want to go ahead with this?" Callum asked both his friends.

They both nodded. "Most excitement I've had for ages," said Jinx.

It was more personal for Sophie. "I saw what those guys did to Rose and they are not getting away with it. Besides, who wants to live in a world where everyone is as rude and offensive as they were in the city? Not me, that's for sure."

Callum tried not to let his relief show. He didn't think he had the courage to do this on his own. "Thanks, guys," he said, meaning every word.

Sophie got back to business. "I've checked the train schedules and the passenger services ended at nine-thirty, so we should have a clear run. I also calculated the distance to the outskirts of the city and it's a straight ride down the tracks. It's much quicker than going by road and shouldn't take too long to get there."

Jinx took the bicycles and headed into the woods to hide them. Callum swung out of the Thunderkit so they could attach it to the trolley. He grunted with effort as he pulled his body along the ground to where Sophie was working. Sophie moved towards him but stopped when she saw the look in his eye.

"I can do it," he snapped.

Sophie held out a wrench. "I was just going to give you this."

Callum reddened and took it from her. "Sorry," he murmured.

It was hard work, but before long the trolley was on the tracks with the wheelchair attached.

Sophie then fitted a petrol-driven engine to the rear of her invention. "She won't go fast, but she should go. Let's fire it up."

Callum looked around. "Where's Jinx?"

At that moment the boy reappeared from the woods. His clothes were dishevelled and his face was scratched and bleeding.

"I'm here. A tree fell on me as I was hiding the bikes."

"Are you OK?" asked Callum.

"Yeah, fine. It was a small tree."

Sophie pulled a twig from his hair. "Some days it must be quite difficult being you."

Jinx sighed. "You have no idea." Then he brightened. "Are we ready to roll?"

"Yep," said Callum. "Let's go."

Callum climbed awkwardly back into his wheelchair and strapped himself in. Sophie picked up her backpack and fastened it to the wheelchair. She threaded an extra-strong strap around the pack, then pulled on it to make sure it was secure. The pack didn't budge. Satisfied, Sophie jumped up behind Callum and positioned herself on a strut next to the engine. Jinx hopped up beside her. She tightened a heavy-duty strap to Jinx's waist and wound it through the back of Callum's chair. Then she did the same for herself.

"Hold on tight, boys," she said as the engine spluttered to life.

The trolley gave a lurch and slowly, but surely, began to chug along the track.

"Woo hoo," yelled Sophie. She punched the air triumphantly.

Callum raised his voice above the sound of the engine. "Nice job, Soph."

Sophie unzipped a pocket in the side of her pack and pulled out three pairs of clear plastic glasses. She put one on herself and handed the other pairs to Callum and Jinx. "Put these on. It'll get a bit windy, and there may be bug splatter."

The boys donned the glasses, just in time too. The trolley was picking up speed and an unwary moth bounced off the side of Callum's left lens.

The engine chugged along and propelled them down the track at some speed. The countryside whipped past, allowing them glimpses of the world at night. Cows and sheep wandered through rolling pastures, owls hooted in the trees and hawks hunted for field mice, their cries haunting in the darkness.

Callum was thankful for the glasses. The wind clawed at his face, and even though his eyes were covered, they still streamed. Sophie and Jinx were more sheltered. They ducked down behind Callum, using the wheelchair as cover. Sophie pulled her phone from her pocket. She'd programmed the route into her maps page and was following their progress.

"Not far now," she shouted to her companions.

"Good." The ride had been fun, but Callum was anxious to get to the warehouse.

He couldn't say afterwards which reached him first: the sound or the vibration. It merged into one long, horrifying realization. The track vibrated, and above the noise of their engine came the rumble of a much larger one. They rounded a bend and saw a large goods train thundering straight towards them.

"Sophie!" yelled Callum. Panic rose in his throat.

Sophie immediately realized her terrible mistake. She'd checked the passenger train timetables but had forgotten about goods trains. Now several hundred tonnes of locomotive were hurtling towards them, and there was no way the train would be able to stop in time. That was assuming the driver had even seen them. As the train bore down upon the trolley, it became clear that he hadn't; there was no wail of warning from the train's horn and no sparks flew from the gigantic metal wheels to indicate that the brakes had been applied.

Callum stared at the train in terror. The locomotive was fitted with a large V-shaped scoop on the front, which was designed to keep the train from being derailed by shunting aside any foreign objects that got onto the tracks. It would easily split Sophie's trolley in two, sweeping them away as casually as an avalanche crushes a sapling.

Time slowed. The train was fifty metres away and closing. A collision was inevitable and it was going to be deadly.

Callum spun around in his chair and screamed at Sophie. "If you're going to do something, do it now."

"I'm with Callum," yelled Jinx. "Now'd be good!"

Sophie barely heard them. She wrenched open

the lid of a clear plastic box that had been welded into the frame of the trolley. A big red button sat in the box. Sophie punched it as hard as she could. Nothing happened.

"I've fitted an eject button, but it's not working," she yelled.

The train was twenty metres away. Its engine growled like a hurricane.

Callum knew he'd never be able to get out of his chair before the train hit them. He was strapped in too tight. Sophie and Jinx might have a chance though. "You two have to get off the trolley. Don't worry about me. Cut yourselves free and jump now," he bellowed.

Jinx yelled back. "We're not leaving you. We'll think of something, won't we, Soph?"

Sophie ignored him. She held tightly to the top of the chair and punched the button again and again. "What's wrong with it?"

Callum glanced at Jinx and saw the thumb on his left hand dancing wildly. He realized his friend's bad luck was jamming the ignition system. He reached over to undo the strap that attached

Jinx to the trolley, but Jinx's weight was pulling against it and the buckle wouldn't budge. Callum yelled to Sophie. "Got a knife?"

Sophie nodded and removed a utility knife from her tool belt, handing it to Callum. He sawed hard and the sharp blade sliced through Jinx's strap.

Jinx stared at him, eyes wide. "What are you doing?"

Callum didn't answer. Instead he grabbed Jinx by the shoulder and threw him from the trolley.

With a cry of surprise Jinx tumbled through the air, then a spectacular spray of water cascaded across the sky as he landed face down in a bog. This was a mixed blessing. It was lucky because the muddy water broke his fall, and unlucky because it was a particularly foul-smelling swamp. At least Jinx was safe.

The same couldn't be said for Callum and Sophie. The train was almost upon them. Callum closed his eyes and braced for impact.

Sophie wrapped herself around the body of the Thunderkit and punched the red button one final time. The ejection system ignited. There was a blinding flash and the wheelchair separated from the trolley and blasted vertically into the night. It flew directly over the nose of the locomotive, clearing its massive metal frame by the narrowest of margins.

The force of the ejection blew the body of the trolley from the tracks. It lifted from the rails then smashed into the iron scoop at the front of the train. There was a loud scraping clang as the trolley was cast aside, its metal frame buckling and twisting as it spun into a ditch beside the railway lines. The train thundered on with barely a scratch on it.

High above the tracks Callum and Sophie hung onto the wheelchair for dear life. If they hadn't been strapped in, the force of the explosion would surely have separated them from the chair. Probably directly into the path of the train.

Sophie prayed aloud. "Please let stage two of the ejection sequence work." She reached for the pack she had attached to the Thunderkit and pulled a cord on its side. A large colourful parachute spat out, blooming above them. The wheelchair swung wildly beneath the chute then settled as they dropped towards the ground.

Callum couldn't believe his eyes. He stared at the parachute billowing above them. "Where on earth did you get that?"

Sophie slumped against Callum's wheelchair and ran a hand through her hair, relief painted on her face. "Army surplus. They used to drop jeeps with this chute. I figured it'd work just as well for a couple of kids and a wheelchair."

Callum shook his head in amazement. "That was one hell of a fail-safe device."

"Yep, I based it on a jet fighter ejection seat. I rigged some charges to blow through the catches on the trolley and blast us into the air. The only problem is the explosion probably warped the trolley base, which might make it difficult to repair for the trip home."

Callum stared at Sophie, incredulous. "You see that as the only problem?"

Sophie looked at the rapidly approaching earth. "Well, that, and the landing."

# TWELVE

Callum's wheelchair tipped over when it hit the ground, but the impact was surprisingly gentle. The wind was light and the chute dragged Sophie and Callum a few metres then deflated. They also had the good fortune to land in a field that contained only a few freaked-out cows.

Once they'd stopped moving, Sophie drew her knife and cut the parachute lines. She also sliced through the straps holding both her and Callum to the wheelchair. Callum fell sideways onto the ground and lay still. Sophie was beside him immediately. "Are you hurt?"

Callum flashed a look of panic. "Oh my God, I can't feel my legs."

"That's not funny." Sophie punched him in the arm. "I'm serious."

Callum grinned. "For someone who has just been blasted over the nose of a speeding train, I'm extremely well. You?"

"A few bruises, ribs are a bit sore, but pretty good." She burst out laughing. "I can't believe that worked."

Callum found himself laughing too. "An ejection seat! What were you thinking?"

"What about you? What did you do to Jinx?"

"I had to get him off the trolley. I hope he's OK."

Sophie pointed to a bedraggled figure tromping through the field. "Here he comes now. Why don't you ask him?"

Jinx squelched up to his friends and dropped onto the ground beside them. He was covered in mud and smelled like a rotten egg.

Callum began to speak. "Jinx, I'm s—"

Jinx stopped him with a wave of his hand. "No

need to apologize. My stupid bad luck was messing with the firing mechanism, wasn't it?"

Callum nodded.

"Thought so. Sorry about that." He sighed deeply. "I'll just head home then, eh?"

"What! No. Don't be dumb," exclaimed Callum. "We need you."

He hoped Sophie would back him up. She did.

"Yeah, we still need a lookout. You're part of the team."

Jinx grinned. "You mean it?"

"'Course," said Callum. "You'll have to stay downwind though."

Sophie held her nose. "It's like a combination of sour milk, old tennis shoes and dog vomit."

Jinx grabbed a handful of grass and wiped off as much of the mud as he could. "Mum's gonna have a fit."

Callum pulled himself to his wheelchair and climbed aboard. "Right," he said. "We can't sit around here all night chatting. We've got a job to do. I'll just run a few checks on my chair."

He rocked the Thunderkit, clicked it into

out mode and then gingerly wheeled along the grass. The carbon-fibre frame was scratched but undamaged. He spun the chair around in a three-sixty-degree turn. It was fine.

Sophie handed Jinx her backpack. "Grab the chute."

Jinx ran over to the parachute, which had wrapped itself around a nearby bush. He folded it into a neat bundle and placed it into Sophie's pack, then handed it back to her. "Any idea where the warehouse is?"

"Close, I think. If we follow the railway tracks for another few hundred metres, we should be sweet." Sophie referred to her phone. "I'd like to find the trolley first though. That's our ride home."

Sophie, Jinx and Callum worked their way back along the train tracks. They located the trolley lying in a twisted heap beside the rails. One look at the mangled wreckage and it was clear it was destroyed beyond repair. Two of the four wheels were missing and the main support struts had snapped and warped. The engine wasn't anywhere to be seen.

Callum shuddered. If things had gone differently, he and Sophie could easily have been lying amongst the mess.

Sophie kicked the remains of the trolley with her shoe. "We won't be going anywhere on that. Guess we'll have to find another way home."

Callum tried not to show his relief. He'd gone right off travelling by rail.

The trio approached the rear of the car parts warehouse. They waited behind some trees where they had a good view of the back of the building. "Can I have the binoculars?" Callum asked Jinx.

Jinx passed a powerful set of field glasses to Callum. He pushed aside a branch and swiftly scanned the surroundings. "No one in the sentry box, but there's a camera on the corner nearest the garage and the dog run goes right around the back.

"Pretty much what we expected then," said Sophie.

Callum agreed. "Yeah. OK, we stick to the plan." He handed the binoculars back to Jinx. "I'll black out the camera, Jinx watches for guards, and Soph sorts out the dog."

They all took their positions. Jinx wriggled forwards on his stomach and hid himself under a large leafy bush.

Callum rolled cautiously forwards until he sat at the edge of the tree line. Sophie followed close behind. When he was happy with his spot, Callum reached into his wheelchair bag and withdrew a collapsible paintball gun. He unfolded the barrel and stock, then screwed a gas canister into the rear of the gun. Callum loaded several balls of black paint into the chamber and cocked the weapon. He pushed the stock of the gun hard into his shoulder, took aim and fired. The weapon spat twice, and two gleaming balls sped through the night air, slamming directly into the lens of the surveillance camera, covering it with a thick layer of black paint.

"Nice shot," said Sophie.

A smile played over Callum's lips. He flicked on the gun's safety catch and laid the weapon on his lap. "Your turn."

Sophie crept beyond the tree line and scanned the area. "Looks clear. Cover me. I'll signal you when I'm done."

Callum nodded. Jinx whistled a pre-assigned bird call – a warbling twitter. This was a signal of acknowledgement. He'd been given one further call – an owl hoot – which he was to use as a warning of impending danger. He had practised his owl impression and was secretly pleased with the result.

Without looking back, Sophie tightened the straps on her backpack and melted into the night. She moved furtively, making it to the wire fence at the rear of the warehouse without incident. She dropped to one knee, unclipped the pack that contained the parachute and dumped it onto the ground in front of her. She reached into a compartment near the bottom of the pack and withdrew a clear plastic container holding two chunks of rump steak. Sophie clicked the lid off and removed a piece of meat stuffed with fast-acting sleeping pills. She tossed the drugged meat over the top of the fence and into the dog run.

Her timing was immaculate. Seconds later the German shepherd that had previously tried to amputate her fingers rounded the corner and raced towards her, lips curled in a vicious snarl. Sophie jumped back from the fence. She hoped the dog would notice the meat before it launched into a fit of barking. Fortunately, the dog's stomach won out and it wolfed down the steak like a four-legged eating machine or a golden retriever.

Sophie threw the second piece of meat over the fence and watched as the dog downed it just as rapidly. The dog licked its lips, sniffed the ground and walked over to the wire directly in front of Sophie. It regarded her with a calculating gaze. Clearly it was prepared to work for food – it would keep quiet as long as Sophie kept the meaty treats coming. Sadly she was out of steak.

The dog watched as Sophie made a show of rummaging around in her backpack. In desperation she pulled out an apple and threw it over the fence. The German shepherd dashed after the piece of fruit, sniffed it in a disparaging way then came back to Sophie, snarling with disappointment.

The animal was clearly a strict carnivore.

"Come on, pills," implored Sophie. She knew the dog would soon realize she was out of food and it would revert to being the guard hound from hell.

The dog opened its mouth but instead of barking, it yawned. Then its eyes glazed over and it dropped to the ground. Within seconds the dog was snoring loudly.

Sophie sighed with relief then retrieved a pair of wire-cutters from her pack. She returned to where Callum waited in the bushes and waved.

Callum wheeled over to Jinx and gave him the paintball gun. "Patrol the rear of the warehouse. If you see anything suspicious or the dog wakes up, call Soph's phone. If we're not back in two hours, call the police." He patted the gun. "This is for emergencies only."

"OK," whispered Jinx. "Are you sure you don't want me to come with you?"

"No. You're our backup. We need you here."

Jinx gave an enthusiastic nod. He was backup. That meant he was their last line of defence. How cool was that!

Callum left Jinx and wheeled to the fence as fast as he could. By the time he arrived, Sophie had already cut a large hole in the wire.

Sophie dumped her backpack behind a bush. She wanted to move freely once they got inside the run. Callum and Sophie sneaked through the hole, hugged the wall of the warehouse and edged their way along the side of the building. Before long they were directly outside the doorway Sophie had seen the previous day, but this time the door was shut and locked. Fortunately, a large dog flap had been built into its wooden frame.

"I'll go in through the dog door and then let you in," Sophie said in a soft voice.

"Be careful."

Sophie pushed open the dog flap with her hand, popped her head through and peered inside. The room was gloomy, cramped and smelled heavily of dog. The concrete floor was strewn with chewed dog bones and grubby stuffed toys in various states of disembowelment. A dog bed lay against a far wall. Beside it were two bowls. The dog's name had been engraved in them. It was called Ripper.

Sophie fervently hoped the sleeping pills would last a long, long time.

The rest of the room was empty. A closed wooden door was fitted in the opposite wall. Sophie assumed the door led into the factory. She listened for sounds of movement, heard nothing and crept inside.

Sophie wrinkled her nose; the dog smell was even stronger inside the room. She examined the door she'd just crawled through. It was secured by a bolt. She slid it back and let Callum in. Sophie moved to the door that led to the warehouse. Callum signalled for her to come close.

Sophie padded over to him and crouched down beside his chair. Callum whispered, "Is the tracking device still working?"

Sophie took out her phone and checked. "Yeah, the signal's weak. The battery must be dying. I can't pinpoint it, but it's definitely coming from somewhere inside this building."

"I just wanted to double-check. Right, here's what I think we should do. This is the point of no return. We are now officially breaking and entering. Going into the warehouse could be dangerous, so I'll go in alone and see what I can find. You join Jinx and wait for me outside."

Sophie was quiet for a few seconds before answering. "OK, good suggestion, but I've got a better one: we totally ignore your plan, because frankly it's rubbish. Then we go into the warehouse together, get your gran's goodness back, destroy the stupid bad bomb and go home—"

"But…" interrupted Callum.

"Do you really think I'm going to let you have all the fun?"

Callum folded his arms across his chest. "I can do this on my own, you know."

"Of course you can, but why would you when I'm here?"

Callum shook his head and forced a smile. "You really are the most annoying girl in the world."

"That's probably true."

Sophie gave him a wink then pulled the handle and opened the door to the warehouse.

# THIRTEEN

The door opened directly into a cavernous loading bay. Moonlight flooded in from a skylight and through several heavily barred windows. The warehouse was silent and dark. Its concrete floor was blackened from the tyre marks of hand trolleys and forklifts that roamed busily around during the day. At night the lifting equipment sat idle at one end of the loading bay. Large elevated shelving units lined the walls and formed a series of aisles. The shelves sat on sturdy wooden legs with the first platform beginning about three metres above the ground then progressing upwards in layers about two metres apart, stretching almost to the ceiling. Each unit was filled with a myriad of boxes and pallets. Foreign markings were printed on many of the containers. Callum guessed the boxes held car parts. At first glance everything seemed above board.

Callum clicked his wheelchair to in mode and wheeled through the aisles looking for anything to indicate that the warehouse wasn't what it seemed. Sophie shadowed him, her eyes scanning the darkened corners of the loading bay for movement.

An open door near the rear of the warehouse caught Callum's eye. He rolled cautiously towards it and stopped before the doorway. He glanced inside. The room was poorly lit, but he could make out the shapes of several vehicles lined up in the gloom. He motioned for Sophie to join him.

"This looks like the garage. Let's see if the van you saw outside my aunt's house is in here."

Sophie removed a torch from her tool belt. Five vehicles were parked in the dark: a late model dark grey Mercedes, a compact, well-used runabout, two white vans with Big Al's Used Car Parts painted on the side and a black van with tinted windows. Sophie covered the torch with her hand to restrict its beam and slipped towards the vehicles. "I think this is the van, but I can't be sure."

Callum nodded. "Let's see what else we can find."

Sophie panned the torch around the garage. They spotted nothing of real interest so they went through an internal doorway that led directly into an office.

The room was tidy and organised. A sleeping computer sat on an expensive desk. The desk also held a set of in and out trays holding two neatly stacked piles of paper. Resting against the desk was a comfortable chair. Two doors were nearby. One led back into the loading bay and the other to another office.

Sophie walked towards the second office. "I'll take this one."

Callum began sifting through the papers in the trays. He was strangely calm, too focused on the task at hand to be afraid. He was, however, well aware of the urgency of their mission. They needed to move fast.

The papers in the tray revealed little; apart

from discovering that the auto parts business was extremely lucrative, Callum found nothing out of the ordinary.

Sophie's rifling of the secretary's office brought about similar results. After ten minutes of fruitless searching, Sophie and Callum returned to the loading bay.

Callum banged the arm of his wheelchair in frustration. "I feel like we're missing something."

Sophie cast her eyes over the rows of shelves. "I know what you mean. Do you think it's worth checking one of those boxes?"

Callum shrugged. "Maybe. They're a long way off the ground though. I'm not sure how we'd get to them."

"I am," said Sophie as she leaped onto a forklift. She started the electric engine. "I've always wanted to drive one of these."

"Be careful," warned Callum. "I've heard they are difficult to drive."

"Not a problem," said Sophie, confidently, as the forklift lurched backwards and collided with a wooden pallet that had been leaning against the warehouse wall. The pallet fell over and a thunderous crash echoed through the building.

Callum screwed up his face and waited for some sort of response, but the warehouse remained quiet.

"Sorry," whispered Sophie in her softest voice, which was a little redundant after the racket she'd just made.

She hopped off the forklift and inspected the damage to the pallet.

"Callum, come here," she hissed urgently.

Callum hurried to the rear of the forklift. The pallet had fallen aside to reveal the entrance to a goods elevator. The lift was big enough for three or four grown men to stand in and was surrounded by a mesh cage.

"Look what I found," said Sophie, behaving as if the accident was completely planned. "Wonder where it goes."

Callum pulled open the elevator door and rolled inside. "Only one way to find out."

Sophie jumped in after him and shut the door. A button on the wall indicated their movement choices – up or down. Callum pushed the down button and the elevator whirred to life with a disconcerting jolt.

It was a short trip to the lower level of the warehouse. At first there was little to see but concrete floor, then the basement level of the warehouse came into view. A walkway spanned a wide drain that traversed the length of the building. A fast-moving stream of water flowed through it. Beyond the drain was a training area that would have looked more at home in a martial arts gym. Olive-green mats were stacked in a neat pile beside racks of weights. Padded, sweat-stained benches were lined up on the wooden floor like hurdles on a running track. At the far end of the training area was a closed wooden door.

Directly to the right of the elevator was a barred cage, which could obviously be used as a holding cell. Two lumpy, stained mattresses and a bucket were the only contents of the prison. To the left of the lift was an entranceway that led to a dark room. The area was dimly lit. Callum could just make out two pairs of black combat boots sitting outside the doorway. He figured the room was for Lester's thugs. Both Callum and Sophie had the impression they had descended on a military compound.

"It doesn't look much like Big Al's Used Car Parts any more," Callum whispered. "But it does look like the kind of place those bullies we met at my aunt's house would live."

Sophie quietly slid the elevator door aside and the two friends moved onto the walkway that crossed the drain. Callum looked down into the black water sluicing beneath him. The watercourse was deep and foreboding. "And this drain is just plain weird."

Sophie wasn't going to argue. Being underground made her uncomfortable. She drew in a deep breath to push through her claustrophobia. She opened a pouch on her tool belt and checked her home-made smoke bomb and concussion ball. They were fine, and having some means of defence close to hand comforted her. It wasn't just the enclosed space that was a cause for concern. She could still picture the slick black Glock pistol in the hands of the solidly built thug. She had no desire to have the same barrel pointed at her.

Callum and Sophie's first move was to check the room where they thought Lester's thugs would be housed. Naturally, they didn't want to get too close, so they stayed in the shadows until they were near enough to listen through the door. A rhythmic snoring came from within. Satisfied no one was stirring, they crossed the drainage ditch via another walkway and crept back the way they'd come.

Callum pointed to the door at the end of the training area. "Let's check out that room."

Sophie nodded. They made their way through the fitness equipment and stopped at the entrance. The door was locked and the room beyond was dark and quiet.

Sophie examined the lock.

"Can you open it?" Callum asked impatiently.

Sophie hunted around on her tool belt and removed a device that looked like a pen light.

"This is pretty cool. It's a miniature laser scanner. It'll map the inside of the lock and give me a reading of what the mechanism looks like so I can work out how to pick it. In theory."

"In theory?"

"Yeah, well, I only invented it yesterday so it's not really tested technology. It should work though."

Callum admired his friend's optimism, especially given her variable hit rate.

Sophie inserted the nib of the scanner into the keyhole and switched it on. A red light flicked back and forth then issued a beep. Sophie took out her trusty phone and plugged the scanner into the headphone socket. Within seconds a detailed three-dimensional outline of a locking mechanism appeared on the screen. Sophie pulled a bunch of keys from her pouch and flicked through them until she found one that matched the image on the screen. She showed Callum the selected key.

"Try this," she said.

Sophie placed the laser scanner, key ring and the phone back on her tool belt, then inserted the selected key in the lock. She turned it and the door unlocked with a soft click.

"And *that's* how you do it," she said with a smile.

Sophie pushed the door open. Darkness

flooded out like a living thing. Callum and Sophie gathered together at the edge of the doorway, waiting for their eyes to adjust to the gloom.

A deep voice sounded behind them.

"I wouldn't go in there if I were you."

They spun around in shock. Parson and Darryl stood in the middle of the training area. They wore crumpled black tracksuit bottoms, identical olive-green T-shirts and had bare feet. Parson's dreadlocks were matted and stuck to the side of his head. They had just woken up, but this didn't make them any less dangerous. Parson's Glock rested lazily in his hand, pointing at the ground before his feet. Darryl was unarmed but he flexed a biceps the size of a toaster to remind the children that he didn't need to be armed to be dangerous.

Darryl sneered. "Looky here," he said. "It's those brats from the other night. We didn't expect to see you again so soon. 'Specially not in the middle of our top-secret underground hideout."

Parson waved the gun towards the open doorway. "That's the boss's room, and he doesn't like to be disturbed. Lucky for you he's a heavy sleeper. Step back from the door, and we'll let him rest. Let's just keep this between us, eh? "

Panic gripped Callum. He forced himself to stay calm, if not for his own sake, then for Sophie's.

Parson waved the gun at them and hissed through his teeth. "Move."

Callum and Sophie did as they were told. They moved out of the doorway and back into the training area.

Parson spoke again. "The first thing I'd like to know is how you found us."

Callum shrugged and answered with more cool than he felt. "We looked you up in the phone book under 'thugs for hire'."

Darryl stepped forwards threateningly. "Watcha mouth, boy," he snarled.

Callum stood his ground, his fear replaced by anger. They'd come so close; they couldn't fail now. "We're not telling you anything. But I'll give you one chance to return what you stole from my grandmother. If not, things will go very badly for you."

Parson's lips curled into a menacing smile. "You

don't seem to 'ave grasped the situation. I'm the one standin' here with a gun, and my friend Darryl could snap your neck like a cracker if he wanted to, so how 'bout a bit of co-operation?"

"Sorry, no can do." Callum shook his head.

"Doesn't matter. You being here is a bit of a problem for Darryl and me. You see, we told our boss that no one saw us suckin' the goodness out of your gran, so if you're to tell him different, well, let's just say that'll reflect poorly on us." Parson sighed. "So I'm gonna have to kill both of you."

Parson raised his gun. Callum reached for the torch in his wheelchair bag but was too late. Two shots rang out and then there was silence.

# FOURTEEN

Rose woke at 3 a.m. She had a sudden desire to listen to rap music, which was unusual because she hated it. Still, the urge was strong, so Rose got out of bed and strode through her home wearing only her nightgown, flicking on all the lights as she went.

In the kitchen she switched on the radio, tuned it to one of the stations Callum liked and then pumped the volume up until the speakers vibrated against the stereo's plastic casing. While in the kitchen Rose made herself a midnight snack of fried onions and chips. She scoffed it in double-quick time and didn't bother cleaning up the mess.

With the music blaring in the background, Rose went into the living-room and opened the top drawer of the sideboard. Inside were a number of items that had belonged to her late husband, including a cigar box. Rose opened the lid and drew out some matches and a long, fat cigar. She rolled the cigar around in her fingers. She had never smoked and previously thought it was a disgusting habit. Now she had an overwhelming urge to spark one up.

Rose walked through the house, opened the front door and stepped outside, leaving the door ajar. A heavy rock track spilled out into the night. She strode through her front garden and plopped down in an outdoor chair, pulling a second chair over to put her feet on. The metal of the chair legs screeched against the paving stones adding to the cacophony of sound.

Bedroom lights from nearby houses began to wink on as the tranquillity of the evening was violated.

Rose lit the cigar, exhaled a curtain of heavy smoke and reclined in the chair, completely oblivious to the muted complaints of her neighbours. She sighed happily and settled in for a night of obnoxious behaviour.

Jinx checked his watch for the thirteenth time. Sophie and Callum had been gone for one hour and twenty-seven minutes. He'd patrolled the perimeter six times, and so far all he'd seen were a rat and a very big spider (which bit him). He'd also been pooped on by a bird.

Jinx crawled from under the bush where he'd been hiding and ran to a tree closer to the hole Sophie had cut in the wire fence. The dog was still sleeping soundly. It gave the occasional woof in its sleep and its legs pumped comically as it dreamed about chasing cats. Jinx looked at his watch again and came to a decision. It was time Jinx Patterson joined the action.

Two bullets whistled over Callum's and Sophie's heads. The first smacked into Parson's chest and the second caught Darryl in the left shoulder. A burst of red splashed into the air as both men were knocked off their feet. Parson fell hard onto his back, as if punched by an invisible fist, his gun spilling from his hand. Darryl twisted sideways as his balance deserted him. He landed on the floor, legs splayed beneath his body. Both lay still.

Sophie and Callum turned as one and watched in horror as a lean man stepped from the darkness of the room behind them. He was wearing jet-black pyjamas and held a fat pistol loosely in his hand, the barrel still smoking.

His thin lips curled into a smile – not the welcoming kind of smile you'd get from a friend, but the grin a wolf gives its prey seconds before devouring it.

"Visitors. What a pleasant surprise. My name is Lester." He waved at the bodies lying beyond the two children. "These are my associates, Darryl and Parson."

Callum stared at the men on the floor. "Are they…"

"Dead?" finished Lester. "No, probably not.

I shot them with reduced-velocity training ammunition. The bullets are filled with a water-soluble coloured marking compound. They pack a punch at close range but aren't normally fatal."

A groan from Parson confirmed Lester's diagnosis.

Lester opened the chamber of his gun with a flick of his wrist and ejected the spent cartridges. They fell onto the floor with a dull clang. "The police and army use them to make indoor training exercises more realistic. I do the same, but sometimes I fire a little closer than recommended. It reminds my staff that I can't abide disobedience."

Lester held out the hand that wasn't carrying the gun. It was clenched in an upturned fist. He opened his fingers and sitting in his palm were six copper-jacketed bullets. "These, however, are the real thing." He fed the ammunition into the empty chambers of the pistol then flicked it shut. "So I suggest you do exactly what I tell you."

Lester trained the gun on Sophie and Callum. Edging past them, he retrieved Parson's pistol from the floor. He slid it into the waistband of his pyjama bottoms. "I don't know how you found me or why you are here, but you're going to regret trespassing on my property."

Callum snapped at the man. "We know your thugs sucked the goodness out of my grandmother and that you've got it hidden here – and so do the police. So if you don't give it back to me right now, you'll be in big trouble."

"My, my, you two are quite the detectives," said Lester. "But if you had told the police, they'd already be here – either that or they didn't believe you, which is much more likely. Who's going to believe a couple of brats' far-fetched stories about brain-sucking machines? I do wonder if you came here alone though. Tell me, can I expect to find any other little people ferreting about in my warehouse?"

Jinx was their only hope of rescue now. It was vital Callum protected his friend. "It's just us," lied Callum.

Lester looked at the boy long and hard then shifted his gaze to Sophie. "Is that right, young lady? Is it just you and the cripple?"

Sophie held his stare, her voice ice-cold. "Yes, and he's disabled, not crippled."

"You're a feisty young thing," laughed Lester. "I like that. But I also think you and your *disabled* friend are not telling me the truth."

Lester kicked Parson and Darryl hard in the legs. "Come on, you two. Get up. I'm not going to shoot you again. Well, probably not anyway."

Parson let out another moan and pulled himself into a sitting position. He had a large splatter of red paint in the middle of his chest. Darryl rolled over and drew himself into a similar position, grimacing with every movement. Paint smeared his left side.

Parson coughed and shook his head, clearly disorientated. He spoke in a halting voice. "We're real sorry, Boss. We was gonna tell you about the kids but—"

"But what?" interrupted Lester. "You thought you'd leave them wandering around as witnesses? The reason I ask you to tell me everything is so we don't end up with a situation like this." Lester swung his gun and pointed it at Parson's head.

"Perhaps I will shoot you after all. Or should I just throw you both into the drain?"

Parson fired a look at the watercourse behind him and shuddered. "Please, Boss, not that. We'll do anything." Darryl nodded in agreement. "Anything." They were more frightened of the drain than the gun.

Callum couldn't contain his curiosity. "What's so scary about the drain?"

Lester kept the gun trained on his henchmen. "It's not so much the drain, but where it leads. It empties straight into the aptly named Shark Bay. So even if they survived the churning waters of the culvert, it's unlikely they'd last long against a hungry great white. Terrible way to go, all that thrashing, screaming and tearing. Mind you, bullets aren't a barrel of laughs either."

Lester pointed his gun directly at Sophie. "As you'll soon discover, if you don't take your hand out of there."

While Lester was talking, Sophie had slowly moved her hand to her tool belt and was reaching for the concussion ball. A few more seconds and she would have had it.

Lester waved the gun in a circular motion, never taking his eyes off Sophie. "Take the belt off and throw it here."

Sophie had no choice. She unbuckled her tool belt and tossed it to Lester. He ran an appreciative eye over the tools and weapons hanging from the belt. "Impressive," he muttered.

Lester adjusted the tool belt and put it around his waist, then gave his attention to his henchmen. "I'm going to give you both one more chance. Go check the warehouse and the perimeter. If you find anyone snooping around, bring them to me."

Relief flooded through Darryl and Parson. They got gingerly to their feet. "Yes, Boss. Right away, Boss," said Parson. The two thugs hobbled towards the elevator.

Lester watched them leave and shook his head. "It's hard to get good help."

He returned to Callum and Sophie. He waved them into the dark room, then moved quickly in behind and switched on the light.

The room was sparsely furnished. It was

dominated by a large bed, which would have dwarfed the man who slept in it. All his bed linen was black. Creepy.

A solid metal door stood beside the bed. It was controlled by an electronic keypad.

Lester herded them towards the door, excited. "Since you've made all this effort to find me, I'm going to show you something no one else has ever seen – my laboratory."

Lester punched four numbers into the keypad. Five, three, seven, two. Callum watched carefully, committing the numbers to memory.

"There's no point memorizing my code; you'll only ever be in this room once." Lester smiled condescendingly at the boy.

The latch released with a slow whirr as three large metal rods retracted into the wall cavity. The door slid aside. The lighting in the room was dull. Patches of green light danced across the floors, walls and ceilings like blobs in a gigantic lava lamp. The air pulsed.

"Go in," hissed Lester from behind Sophie and Callum.

They entered with a mixture of curiosity and fear. Callum gulped as he saw the wall tank filled with thousands of squirming, oozing blobs of goodness. His eyes met Sophie's and they both gasped as they realized what they were looking at.

"Ugly little things, aren't they?" sneered Lester.

Callum shook his head. "They're beautiful."

Sophie stood transfixed by the fluorescent blobs writhing in the aquarium. She moved closer to the glass and placed a hand against the tank. A shudder ran through her body as if she could feel the frustration of the creatures imprisoned within. "It hurts them to be separated from their owners; they're suffering."

"Rubbish," scoffed Lester. "They're just blobs of matter. They don't have feelings, and even if they do, it's of no consequence. They're redundant anyway. Who cares about goodness any more?"

Callum rounded on Lester. "I do, and I won't let you set off your bomb."

Lester's eyes narrowed. "How could you possibly…"

He wrenched open Sophie's tool belt and

rummaged around, withdrawing her phone. He clicked through the settings until he found the scanner and switched it on. The battery was running low and the signal was fading but clearly came from within the room. Lester spun around wildly, searching for the source. His eyes fell on the brain scanner case, and he strode over to it, running his hands over the aluminium body. Within seconds he had located Sophie's bug. He examined it with a practised eye then, to Callum's and Sophie's surprise, burst out laughing.

"Tracking and audio. Genius!" He spoke to his captives. "I should offer you both jobs. You could be my apprentices in a brand-new world." Lester's eyes took on a fanatical glint as he spoke. "Think of it. I'm going to create a society not bound by manners, rules and other people's opinions of what's 'right'. With no more goodness in the world we can do and say what we like – no restrictions, no boundaries, no judgement. I'm giving everyone their freedom. In years to come people will see me as a hero. And you could be by my side."

Callum glared at the man. "No, thank you.

We've seen what your world would be like. It'll be full of people who don't care about anything or anyone other than themselves. I'd rather die than be part of it."

Lester sighed with disappointment. "I expected as much. You're both too clogged up with morals and scruples to see my vision. Oh, well, your loss. So what shall I do with you now?"

"You can start by giving me my grandmother's goodness back," Callum said with soft menace.

Lester clapped his hands together. "What, and give up the pride of my collection? That's not going to happen. I can show you it though – it's quite impressive."

Lester walked to his workbench, picked up the remote control and pushed a button. A large rocket rose from the bench. Encased in the body of the rocket was a clear Perspex vacuum flask containing Rose's golden goodness. Energy crackled around the edge of the globe. Callum noticed the rocket was plugged into the power supply.

"Behold, the world's one and only bad bomb," proclaimed Lester, theatrically. "It'll be fully charged in a few hours." Lester pointed to a cylindrical shaft that penetrated the ceiling of the laboratory and led outside. "Once it's in the exit chute, its thrusters will fire and blast it into the Earth's atmosphere, then the charge will detonate, and *BAM*, a world completely devoid of goodness."

Callum pulled on the rims of his wheelchair and started towards the bench. Lester was on him with surprising speed. He grabbed the wheelchair and held Callum back, pressing the pistol into his ribs for emphasis. "Now, now," he chided. "Let's not do anything stupid."

Callum wrestled against Lester's grip but couldn't break it. He twisted his body to face the man. "Let me go," he spat.

Lester gave him a sad smile. "I don't think so. I have plans for you and your friend."

Callum tensed. "What are you going to do?"

"Why, I'm going to use the brain sucker on you." Lester looked at him, genuinely surprised. "What did you expect?"

# FIFTEEN

Jinx crept quietly past the sleeping German shepherd. He wasn't sure how long it would remain asleep, but he prayed it would be a few minutes more. As he drew level with the dog, it lifted its huge head, bared its fangs and let out a low, rumbling growl.

Just my luck, thought Jinx as he ran for it, sprinting as fast as his legs would carry him. The dog struggled to its feet, still woozy. It shook its head and its eyes cleared. Within seconds it had fully recovered, and it took off after Jinx, growling with indignation. Jinx could hear the dog's snapping jaws just behind him, and he put on a final burst of speed then threw himself head first through the dog door. He rolled when he hit the ground and scrambled into the warehouse, slamming the door behind him.

Jinx bent over and sucked in a deep lungful of air, breathing hard. He straightened and looked directly into Parson's grinning face. Darryl stood beside him. Before he could react, Parson grabbed him by the arm and shook him.

"Are there any others?" the man roared into his face.

Jinx said nothing. He struggled but couldn't shift the man's grip.

"Have a look outside," Parson said to his companion, and the big man left. Jinx was roughly searched, and his mobile phone and paintball gun were taken.

Before long Darryl returned. "Better get him to the boss," he grunted when he got back. Parson nodded and Jinx was flung over his shoulder like an old overcoat.

As they carried him through the warehouse, Jinx's left thumb began to spasm. Suddenly, a stack of pallets on one of the shelves above them began to tremble. Jinx watched as the pallets juddered closer and closer to the edge of the shelf. He glanced at his captors to see if they'd noticed – they hadn't. Jinx braced himself for impact as the pallets tumbled over the edge and hurtled towards them. The men caught sight of the falling pallets at the last second and reacted with speed. Parson threw the boy to the floor and raised his arms to protect himself. The pallets smashed into the men and all three bodies crashed to the ground, splintered planks littering the floor around them.

Jinx lay hunched in a ball on the floor, protected from the falling pallets by the biggest thug, who had collapsed on top of him. This made escape impossible, but he was happy to be under the bulky body when the insects attacked. A swarm of bees had made their nest in one of the pallets, and now they set about punishing the people who disturbed them. The two men leaped from the smashed remains of the pallets, yelling in pain and jumping around, completely engulfed in a stinging mass of agitated bees.

Jinx also got to his feet, making the most of the diversion. He ran for the exterior door, only to find the German shepherd barring his way. He went back into the warehouse and looked for a way out. All the exits were blocked by either psychotic dogs or angry bees. As he studied his surroundings, he formulated a plan and climbed onto a nearby forklift.

Right, he reasoned. I'll drive this forklift through the wall and escape that way.

He turned the key and the machine burst into life, briefly. Almost immediately Jinx's bad luck caused something to go wrong. With a sudden screech and a fart of black smoke, the engine exploded. The smoke drifted over the swarm of bees and calmed them down. Jinx stared at the angry dog now circling his forklift and glanced towards the badly stung men emerging from the cloud of dropping bees. He moaned in frustration and sat in the cab of the broken forklift waiting to be recaptured.

After leaving the laboratory, Lester trooped Sophie and Callum through the training area and over the drainage ditch to the punishment cells he had built beside the elevator.

Lester opened the cell door. He grabbed Callum's wheelchair and pushed him inside, then slammed the door shut. He took hold of Sophie's wrist, holding her back.

"Get your hands off me," cried Sophie, struggling against him.

Callum slammed his wheelchair into the door. "Leave her alone," he yelled.

Lester sneered and shook his head. "I've got a lot to do this morning so I only have time to suck the goodness out of one of you. I thought it'd be fun to attach the brain sucker to the girl and make you watch."

"Take me instead," Callum said, and then added in a voice only Lester could hear, "Hurt her, and I'll destroy you."

Something in Callum's tone chilled Lester. He almost believed the boy. He gathered himself and decided it didn't matter whose goodness he took. Besides, he wanted to humiliate the boy for having the audacity to threaten him. He gave a dry laugh. "Say please."

Callum held Lester's gaze. "Please," he said quietly.

Lester regained some of his confidence. "How about 'pretty please'?"

"Pretty please," said Callum in a clear voice.

"Such lovely manners. Well, let's change that." Lester wrenched the door open and threw Sophie roughly inside. She fell to the floor. Callum reached over to help her up. Sophie took his hand and clambered to her feet. "You don't have to do this," she whispered, brushing angry tears from her eyes.

"Yes, I do," replied Callum. "This is all my fault. It's *my* gran who had her goodness removed, not yours. I should never have got you involved. Now look at the mess we're in. I'm so sorry, Soph."

Sophie shook her head. "You don't have to be. I knew the risks when I decided to help, and I don't regret it. When are you going to realize that you don't have to do everything by yourself?

Friends help each other no matter what."

"You're right," he murmured. "And now I'm helping you."

He wheeled out of the cell and let Lester take hold of his chair.

Sophie screamed at Lester. "You can't do this!"

Lester raised a quizzical eyebrow. "You'd be amazed at what I can do."

He reached for a brass key hanging on the wall beside the elevator. He locked the cell door then put the key back on the hook.

"Now the fun begins," he said, addressing Sophie. "And you'll be able to watch it all from the safety of your cell."

Lester pushed Callum back over the drainage ditch and into the training area. He positioned Callum's wheelchair in front of one of the benches, about twenty metres from the cell and facing directly towards Sophie. Lester moved behind the boy and pulled the brake on his wheelchair. "Don't want you running away, do we?" He poked the boy's legs then added cruelly, "Oh that's right, you can't."

Lester walked back into his laboratory and returned with a silver case. He placed the case on a nearby workout bench and snapped it open. With almost reverential care Lester lifted a gleaming aluminium vacuum pump and flask from the case. It was similar to the machine that Sophie and Callum had witnessed Parson using on Rose, but it was older and chunkier.

He paraded the machine in front of Callum. "I'm going to use a very special machine on you. This is the first manners-extraction machine I ever invented – the Mark One Brain Sucker. It works extremely well; in fact, if anything, it's a little too efficient. Not only does it suck out your goodness, but it also removes a small chunk of your brain. The convenient side effect being that your memory will be completely wiped. But don't worry, you're just a kid so you won't forget anything of any importance."

Callum ignored Lester's taunt. His muscles tensed as he prepared to launch himself from his chair.

Without warning, Lester wrapped one of

his arms around Callum's chest and pinned him in place. He was much stronger than he looked. "Give me any trouble, boy, and I'll put a bullet in you." Callum relaxed, but Lester didn't release him, instead he pressed harder. Callum gasped.

Sophie saw what was happening from the confines of her cell. "Let him go, you sick freak," she screamed.

Lester removed his arm from Callum's chest and picked up the brain sucker. He yelled at Sophie, his voice thick with menace. "I'd advise you to keep quiet, young lady, or I might just let the machine keep sucking until there's no brain left at all."

Sophie bit her tongue; she had no option but to watch in silence.

Lester flicked a switch on the side of the vacuum pump, and the machine kicked into life with a low hum. It vibrated violently in Lester's hand. He attached a short hose and a suction cup, then held it close to the boy's head to heighten his fear.

The hairs on the back of Callum's neck stood

on end. He could feel the thrum of the machine as it came closer. The vacuum pump pulled at the air like an exhausted runner gasping for oxygen. Lester clamped his free hand on Callum's shoulder, pushing him hard into the base of the chair. Callum struggled but he couldn't move. He heard Lester's voice, a soft hiss in his ear. "Once your goodness has gone, you'll be just like me."

Then the voice was replaced by a loud *thock* as the suction cup attached itself to Callum's ear. His vision blurred, and his breathing came in short, rasping gasps. His head shook as if it had been placed in a milkshake maker, and there was a roaring within as if an angry beast had been let loose inside his cranium. He smelled burnt onions.

Lester howled with pleasure as he pressed the suction cap tighter onto Callum's ear. It would only be a matter of moments before his goodness let go and was sucked from the boy's skull for ever.

# SIXTEEN

**J**inx offered no resistance as the two badly stung thugs hauled him off the forklift. He was conserving his strength. Both of his captors were considerably worse for wear: their faces were swollen from the bee stings and Parson seemed to have concussion. Jinx was sure he'd soon be free of their clutches, then he'd be able to show Callum and Sophie they had made the right decision including him in the team.

The thugs put him in the service elevator and pushed the down button. Somewhere between the upper and lower floors, the copious amount of poison in the men's bloodstreams overtook them.

Parson was the first to go. Jinx watched happily as the man slumped against the elevator cage and drifted into unconsciousness. Darryl hung on longer, but not much. Woozy and with a face like a puffer fish, he placed one of his massive hands on Jinx's shoulder to steady himself. Jinx shook it off, and the thug joined his friend on the floor of the elevator.

Seconds later the wire cage cleared the concrete lip of the floor above and the underground lair opened up before Jinx. He assessed the situation. His friends were in grave danger, of that there was no doubt. Sophie was locked behind the metal bars of a cramped and, frankly, quite unsanitary-looking cell, but she seemed unhurt. It was Callum who was in the most trouble.

Jinx had no idea who the thin man was, but recalling Callum's description of the brain-sucking machine, he could guess what the man was doing.

Rage coursed through Jinx's body, not an uncontrollable anger, but a cold focused fury. He looked over the unconscious forms of the goons on the elevator floor and knew they were no further threat. Then he let out a loud warbling hoot. This was the signal he, Callum and Sophie had agreed on earlier, but this time he wasn't warning his friends of danger – he was warning his enemies that he was coming. He opened the elevator door and stepped onto the concourse. Sophie scrambled as close to him as she could and yelled through the bars: "Run, Jinx. Get out of here."

But Jinx wasn't going anywhere. He was going to help his friends no matter what. The thumb on his left hand started to shake, and he concentrated all his attention on the machine in the thin man's hands. Jinx raised his own hand and pointed at his enemy. The shake spread from his thumb and soon his whole arm was vibrating.

All of a sudden the machine attached to Callum's ear began to smoke, and then it whined like an abandoned dog. The machine sparked and sent a jolt of electricity coursing along the thin man's arm. The man jumped in alarm, dropping the machine onto the ground. The suction cup was wrenched from Callum's ear, uncoupling with a wet pop.

Sophie stared at Jinx in disbelief. His entire left-hand side was vibrating now, but his eyes were sharp and clear.

"Jinx," she cried urgently. "What's happening?"

The red-headed boy turned to her, his face breaking into a wide smile. "I'm controlling it," he replied with a crazy laugh. "I'm controlling the bad luck. For once in my life it's working for me."

The bars under Sophie's hands began to shake. Softly at first, then more violently. The floor was trembling too. A low rumble echoed through the chamber as the entire facility began to quake.

"Whoa," bellowed Jinx. "Not good." He was flailing around like a sock in a tumble-dryer. His eyes were wild. "Soopphhiiiieeee," he hollered. "I don't think I'm in control any more."

The underground lair became a living thing: the walls shuddered, the floor heaved and plaster rained down as great cracks appeared in the ceiling. Sophie was flung to the floor of her cell. Her hip struck something hard and a shock of pain shot through her body. Shards of cement smashed into the bars above her, and she threw her arms up to protect her head from the falling debris.

Jinx fell to his knees. His convulsing had stopped, but the earthquake he'd brought on continued. Jinx crawled as close as he could to Sophie. He shouted through the bars, trying to be heard over the cacophony of crashes and cracks that filled the chamber. He rattled the cell door. "I'll get you out of here. Where's the key?"

Sophie pointed to the hook on the wall beside the elevator. The hook was empty. "It was on there."

Jinx scrambled his way across the bucking floor to the wall. He clung to the side of the metal cage with one hand and searched frantically amongst the growing pile of rubble. A glint of brass caught his eye. The key lay half-buried under a layer of cement dust. He reached for it then, just as his fingers touched the metal, a crack opened in the floor and the key disappeared from sight.

Jinx cried with frustration. He glanced back to Sophie and saw the despair in her eyes. He returned to the cell and looked desperately for something to jemmy the door open. He saw nothing. He drew a deep breath and forced himself to calm down. Control, he thought. It's all about control. Jinx focused on the ceiling directly above Sophie's cell. A thin crack opened up. It grew longer and wider as he watched. Cement dropped away revealing a large metal support beam. Jinx focused harder. The beam groaned and shook, and then one end broke free and crashed down on top of Sophie's cell. Large chunks of rock peppered the floor around Jinx, and a boulder the size of an armchair missed him by centimetres. A cloud of dust fell like a curtain, temporarily blacking out everything. Jinx spluttered and lurched towards the fallen beam.

The girder was on a forty-five degree angle, one end still fixed to the ceiling, the other on the floor by the elevator. Tonnes of solid metal had smashed into the ceiling of the cell, bending, twisting and in some places even snapping the bars. Rubble littered the cell floor. Sophie lay amongst the debris. Dust covered her body like a shroud. The girl was still, her eyes closed.

Jinx called her name in anguish. "Sophie!"

She didn't move.

Jinx rattled the bars in panic, shaking the entire cage. "Come on," he screamed. "You're all right, you have to be." He sunk to his knees, head bowed. Then he heard a tiny splutter.

Sophie's eyelids fluttered. She coughed and spat out a mouthful of dust, then drew her body into a crouch.

Jinx hooted with relief and pointed to a section of the cage where the bars had twisted apart enough for her to climb through. "Over here."

Sophie stumbled to the bent bars, and Jinx reached through to help her. As she went to take his hand, a cavernous crack opened beneath Jinx, and he fell onto a narrow outcrop, his body rolling along for several metres then slipping off the edge. At the last possible moment, Jinx grabbed a rock with one hand, saving himself from falling into the darkness below. He grunted with effort as he tried to pull himself back onto the ledge but lacked the strength. "Soph, help!" he called from the cavern.

Sophie squeezed her thin frame through the gap in the cell bars and crept to the edge of the hole. She peered into the darkness and could see the rock walls forming a low tunnel above the ledge where Jinx dangled. A familiar fear gripped her, and she backed away from the tight opening.

Jinx's fingers ached as he clung desperately to the rock. "Hurry, Soph. I can't hold on much longer."

Sophie's heart pounded in her chest. Every nerve in her body was telling her to leave her friends and run to the surface. "I can't do it," she sobbed. Then, with a tremendous effort, she pulled herself together. Sophie took a deep breath and launched herself into the cramped darkness of the hole. Ignoring the cold sweat on her brow and the tightening in her chest, she crawled towards Jinx's dangling body. As his fingers began to slip, she grabbed his wrist. His weight startled her, and she overbalanced, smashing her knees into the dirt to stop from tumbling into the blackness. Breathing hard, she leaned back and pulled Jinx's scrambling form onto the ledge.

"That was close," he huffed. "Now, can we please get out of here?"

She pulled Jinx in the direction of the drainage ditch. "Come on, we've got to find Callum."

Water swirled around the edge of the ditch. The current had swelled to twice its normal flow and the watercourse was at the point of overflowing. Jinx hadn't brought just an earthquake down upon them – he'd summoned a flood as well.

Sophie and Jinx pulled back from the edge and scanned the training area. Callum and Lester were nowhere to be seen.

# SEVENTEEN

**A**s soon as the brain sucker had fallen from Callum's ear, his equilibrium returned. Energy flowed into his body and he reeled back in his chair as if he'd been slapped. His eyes snapped open, his breathing was sharp. He tried to work out what was happening. Had his goodness been sucked away? A test: was it rude to text at the dinner table? Yes! His manners were still intact so he must be all right.

He could still feel Lester's presence behind him, but the thrumming of the machine had stopped. Something had gone wrong. A curse from Lester confirmed his suspicions. Callum tried to turn, but he was still pinned to the chair. He glanced towards Sophie and saw that Jinx was there too. He was just about to call out when the earthquake struck.

In seconds he was surrounded by chaos. The training area erupted as mats, bars and weights were thrown about like autumn leaves. A heavy workout bench flew through the air and smacked into the ground just behind his chair. Callum heard a grunt and the pressure on his shoulder fell away. He was free. Wasting no time, Callum clicked the Thunderkit into out mode and pushed on one rim. The wheelchair spun 180 degrees until he faced Lester's room. He looked for his tormentor and found the thin man lying in a heap against the wall – he must have been clipped by the flying bench.

This was the opportunity Callum had been waiting for. He accelerated hard and manoeuvred deftly around the chunks of masonry and jutting cracks that were appearing in the floor. The suspension in the Thunderkit absorbed a large amount of the floor roll, and Callum moved quickly into Lester's bedroom. He punched the code into the keypad on the laboratory door then wheeled back as it slid open.

The laboratory shook less than the rest of the building. Callum wondered if it had been reinforced. But even so, hairline cracks were appearing in the massive glass aquarium. The blobs of goodness seemed to know something was about to happen. They had clumped together in a gigantic pulsating mass right in the centre of the tank. As Callum watched, the throng thumped against the glass, causing one of the cracks to deepen.

Callum didn't have much time; he didn't want to be in the room when the glass gave way. He saw the bad bomb on the bench and scrambled to wrench it from the power supply when a hand slammed into his wheelchair and pushed him aside. He turned in panic and saw Lester beside the bench. The man must have recovered from the blow and followed him into the lab.

The left side of Lester's head was streaked with dirt and dried blood. He reached for his remote control and sneered. "You're too late, kid." He punched a button and the rocket uncoupled from the power supply. The robotic arm picked up the bomb and moved it towards the launching chute.

Callum knew he had to stop Lester at all costs. The fate of the world's goodness hung in the balance. He acted fast, pulling his torch from its pouch, extending the metal rod and swinging it in a wide arc. The rod caught Lester a glancing blow on the temple, and he crumpled to the ground. Callum returned the torch to its bag. He reached behind him, clicked his new armrest into place, aimed it at the robot and fired the grappling hook. The grapple spun towards the rocket and wrapped around the robotic arm, halting its progress.

A tug of war began as Callum activated the winch. The grapple pulled against the arm as it inched the rocket towards the chute. Almost immediately, Callum's chair rolled forwards, and he slammed on all the Thunderkit's brakes. The chair locked in place, and the battle intensified. The muscles in Callum's arms ached as he gripped the chair's rims to stop it from moving. The winch screamed as the robot tried to pull away. The robot ground to a halt just short of the launch pad, smoke pouring out of its metal joints as it overheated. Its fingers opened, and the rocket dropped onto the bench with a clang. Callum released the brakes and hurtled towards the chute, the winch giving him extra momentum. He grabbed the missile, wrenched it open and took out the flask containing his grandmother's goodness. Then he slammed the tail of the rocket into the bench, bending its fins and ensuring it would never fly.

A sharp crack from the aquarium glass reminded Callum that he didn't have time to waste. He retracted the grapple, tucked the flask safely into his lap and raced across the floor of the laboratory, wheels skidding. He blasted through Lester's room, rocketing over the uneven floor. The going was easier as the quake began to subside. While the building still groaned, no new cracks appeared and masonry had stopped falling from the floors above. Callum wheeled into the training area and immediately caught sight of his friends. They stood on the opposite side of the ditch and looked exhausted but unhurt. Sophie and Jinx saw him at the same time and waved frantically. One single walkway had survived the carnage, and Callum headed for that. Sophie and Jinx began yelling at him, but their words disappeared beneath the thundering of water surging through the drain. As he neared the ditch, Callum triumphantly raised the flask containing Rose's goodness above his head. Then something smashed against the side of his chair. The impact tipped it over and sent him sprawling to the ground.

Lester stood above him, a new cut on his head weeping blood. His odd-coloured eyes burned with hatred. He kicked Callum's wheelchair aside. The Thunderkit fell into a large crack in the floor and wedged there. It rested precariously on the jagged concrete ledge. Lester pulled a pistol from his waistband, raised the gun and pointed it at Callum's chest.

"Give me the golden goodness," he screeched, his voice breaking with rage.

Callum pulled the flask closer to his body. His voice didn't waver. "Never."

Lester's finger tensed on the trigger, then a resounding boom echoed from the laboratory.

Lester turned in time to see a wall of water surging through the doorway. The aquarium had burst. Lester screamed as the water slammed into him like a fist, and he was engulfed in a tidal wave of thousands of writhing fluorescent green blobs. The gun was punched from his hand and it spun across the room, falling into a trench and vanishing from sight. Lester was flung to the ground directly on top of Callum, then the surging mass of water swallowed them both and flushed them into the drainage ditch.

Callum heard Sophie and Jinx yell in horror as he, Lester and the green blobs of goodness disappeared into the swirling waters.

# EIGHTEEN

The churning water in the ditch dragged Callum under for the second time in five minutes. The current was strong and fast, and Callum was already feeling fatigued. He clung desperately to the vacuum flask holding Rose's goodness, but the container made swimming more difficult, and he struggled to get back to the surface. Then, with one final stroke of his powerful arms, Callum broke through and was able to grab a precious gulp of fresh air. He tucked the flask under his shirt to free his arms.

Callum knew it was only luck and his upper-body strength that had kept him alive so far. As he went to draw another breath, he was jerked back under the water. Lester had grabbed his leg and pulled him down. The thin man released Callum's leg and clawed his way up the boy's body, trying to rip the flask from under his shirt. Their bodies smashed together as the waterway coursed into a huge cylindrical pipe. Callum felt the pipe against his back and braced against it before thrusting a hand into Lester's face, pushing as hard as he could. The thin man tumbled away, arms thrashing wildly as he rocketed down a steep section of pipe. Callum pushed for the surface once more and swam fiercely against the current, hoping to put some distance between himself and Lester.

He gained a few seconds respite then plummeted down the pipe like a holiday-maker in a water slide. Callum floated on his back, grabbing a much-needed break. For the first time he was aware of the pulsating green blobs of goodness bobbing along beside him. Several of them glided gently beneath him, they pushed against his body, buoying him up as they rode the tunnels to freedom. The presence of the blobs calmed

Callum, and for a moment he felt as though they were somehow communicating with him, helping him to float as if thanking him for their release. He smiled, knowing the thought was ridiculous, but enjoying it all the same.

All of a sudden the drain opened into a cavern and the water began to boil as the flow increased. Through splashes of water Callum saw something that sent a shudder through his body. Lester was directly ahead. He had managed to grab hold of a feeder pipe and had locked his arm around it. He waited patiently for the current to deliver Callum to him, a look of utter malice on his face. Callum barely had time to react before Lester was on him. The man used his free hand to grasp a handful of Callum's hair and pushed the boy under the water. His face twisted with effort as he held the boy down. Callum struggled, but his flailing arms were unable to break Lester's grip. The man was too securely anchored to the pipe. A heaving tightness enveloped Callum's chest as his lungs cried out for oxygen. His heart pounded in his ears. His vision swirled. He was within seconds of blacking out and then salvation arrived in the form of the smallest and most unexpected of saviours.

Above Callum's drowning body a family of rats, which had been caught in the flood, washed into Lester. The panicked, scurrying rodents scratched at his face and neck in desperation to get out of the water. The youngest one, a female baby no bigger than a cocktail sausage, sank her razor-sharp teeth into Lester's earlobe. The man screamed in pain and thrashed at his face, releasing the pipe and the boy at the same time. With Lester's grip broken, Callum rocketed to the surface. He sucked in a huge lungful of air, then was washed helplessly out the end of the watercourse and launched into the open, about ten metres above a remote inlet. Lester followed seconds later, and he, Callum and thousands of green blobs cascaded along a fountain of water then plunged into the depths of Shark Bay.

Almost immediately, sleek grey fins broke the surface from deep within the cove and glided towards them. Callum was transfixed by the size and speed of the ominous shapes peeling through the water. One fin in particular caught his eye. It was huge, about the size of the sails of a yacht, its edges jagged and scarred – and it was coming straight at him. Callum felt strangely calm. He floated where he had landed, treading water by making slow waving motions with his arms. His body was buoyed further by a group of goodness blobs that had appeared beneath him. It was a pleasant sensation, and Callum relaxed. He knew he couldn't beat the sharks to shore, so he lay back and enjoyed the morning sun on his face. Callum was oddly at peace as the deadly creatures bore down on him.

Lester's reaction was the complete opposite. He had landed further out in the bay, and as soon as he saw the sharks, he screamed in fear and struck out towards Callum and the shore.

Callum leaned his head to one side and watched dispassionately as the huge fin closed in on him. The shark glided through the water, no emotion in its black eyes. It opened its jaws, anticipating the kill. Callum took the flask containing his grandmother's goodness from under his shirt and clasped it to his chest. He closed his eyes and waited to be taken.

Then a weird sensation travelled the length of his body. He felt as if he was being lifted from the water. He opened his eyes and looked around, puzzled. Callum was astounded to see that he *had* been raised from the ocean. A pulsing mass of green surrounded him as hundreds of freed blobs of goodness banded together beneath him like a living island. As more and more blobs joined the group, Callum was gently hoisted aloft. The huge shark dived at the last moment, passing beneath the expanding mass of blobs. The throbbing energy of the green creatures had a strange effect on the sharks, and they backed off, circling in frustration. Then, as one, the living island of goodness began moving Callum towards the shore.

Callum looked back to see if he could spot Lester. The man was just behind the island, swimming desperately for it. Every time he got close, a cluster of blobs would break loose from the main group and force him away, driving him back into the bay and closer to the jaws of the waiting sharks. Lester beat at the blobs with his fists, but they simply bobbed under the blows then reappeared to push against him once more.

Unable to defeat the blobs of goodness, Lester faced the sharks. The desperate man pulled something from around his waist – it was Sophie's tool belt. Suddenly, the ocean directly in front of Lester exploded in a flash of light and a massive column of water burst into the air. A low crump echoed across the bay and a thick black carpet of smoke rolled across the water like an approaching storm, completely obscuring everything in its path. Callum knew instantly what had happened – Lester had set off Sophie's concussion ball and smoke bomb.

When the smoke finally dissipated, about half an hour later, Callum could see nothing. Lester and the sharks were gone and the ocean was flat and still.

The island of goodness gently deposited Callum's exhausted body on the sand at the mouth of the bay. Then it slowly split apart and the blobs began to make their way across the fields to the waterways that would carry them back to the city. From there the mysterious creatures would find their way back to their owners, homing in on individual brainwave patterns that were stored deep in the blobs' memories. In the dark of the night, the blobs would ooze into their owners' bedrooms, slip into their beds and squeeze smoothly back through their ear canals into their brains. Before long most of the inhabitants of the city would have had their stolen goodness completely restored.

As Callum watched the final fluorescent blob melt into the distance, he couldn't help wondering if they had banded together to save him, or if they had just been attracted to the golden glow in the flask he clutched to his chest. He would never really know.

Callum placed the flask on the sand next to his body and dropped his head back onto the sand, exhaustion catching up with him. He raised his hand, looked at his watch and groaned. It was six-thirty in the morning. He had an hour and a half to get back to his gran's house before the welfare people showed up. Even with his wheelchair it was unlikely. Without it, it was impossible. A feeling of despair washed over him. Everything he'd been through would be for nothing if he couldn't restore Rose's goodness. Life away from her was unthinkable. Callum turned his thoughts to Sophie and Jinx; he prayed his friends had made it out of the warehouse uninjured. When he considered their incredible bravery, he felt inspired. Even though his situation was hopeless, he couldn't just give up. He picked up the flask, gritted his teeth and began dragging his body up the beach.

# NINETEEN

Callum had almost made it to the road when he heard the roar of an approaching engine. Seconds later a bright yellow forklift crested a sand dune and sped towards him. Callum laughed with relief as he saw Sophie in the driver's seat. Jinx stood on the forks holding the Thunderkit beside him. He and Sophie had retrieved it from the crack it had fallen into just before the flood. It was battered but still functional.

His friends waved excitedly as they saw him, and Sophie slid the forklift to a stop nearby. Sophie and Jinx raced over as Callum pulled himself into a sitting position. He received a hug from Sophie (which embarrassed both of them) and a pat on the back from Jinx.

After Callum told them what happened, he nodded towards the forklift. "Worked out how to drive it, I see," he said to Sophie.

Sophie smiled. "Yeah, I also added a few extras from the car parts store to pep it up a bit. Including a GPS, which showed us the way to Shark Bay."

"Pep it up a bit," exclaimed Jinx. "The thing's faster than a Formula One car now; it's frightening."

"I'd expect nothing less from Soph." Callum checked his watch. It was seven o'clock. "Will it get us back home in time?"

Sophie sucked air in between her teeth. "It'll be tight."

"We'd better get going then," said Callum with a determined nod.

Sophie wheeled the Thunderkit closer to Callum then she and Jinx stood back, waiting for him to climb aboard. Callum extended his hand. "What are you two standing around for? Help me into the chair."

Sophie and Jinx exchanged a look and beamed.

They grabbed Callum under his shoulders and lifted him easily into the chair. "Just don't make a habit of it," he said with a mock grumble. "Now come on. Let's move."

Jinx shook his head. "You go. The forklift, will be faster with only two onboard."

"But we're a team—"

Jinx cut Callum off. "Yeah, and my job was backup, and I reckon I did that pretty well. Now I'd like to have a rest."

Sophie gave Jinx a wink. "You were an excellent backup man."

"Best ever." Callum wheeled onto the forklift, knowing they didn't have time to argue. "We'll come back for you later."

Jinx sat on the sand and gazed out to sea, smiling to himself. "You'd better."

Sophie climbed into the cab, gunned the engine and drove back to the road. Callum called to Jinx. "Whatever you do, don't go for a swim." Then they roared away.

The forklift pulled up outside Rose's cottage at seven fifty-four exactly. Callum rolled through the gate and was shocked to see his grandmother fast asleep in a garden chair with the stub of a cigar hanging out of her mouth. The front door of the cottage was wide open and music blared from within the house. Sophie was just behind Callum. "You help your grandmother. I'll clean up inside," she yelled as she ran past.

Callum wheeled over to the old lady, careful not to wake her. He took out the flask containing the globe of goodness, unscrewed the lid and placed it on her lap. The globe immediately squeezed out of the tube and climbed to Rose's ear, liquefied and poured back into her head, where it belonged.

Rose woke with a start and spat out the cigar butt. Callum held his breath waiting for her to speak. The old lady looked at Callum for a few seconds then tutted.

"Goodness me, Callum McCullock. You are in quite a state. It looks like no one cares for you, and we can't have that." Rose ran a gentle hand through her grandson's hair then she blinked, looked at herself and blushed bright red. "And look at me, outside in my night attire. Disgraceful. What on earth is going on?"

Relief flooded through Callum. Rose was back to normal. He gave her a huge hug. "No time to explain now, Gran. The welfare people will be here in about five minutes."

Rose gasped and rushed Callum inside. After politely greeting Sophie and thanking her for her assistance, Rose instructed the girl to pop outside and delay the interviewer for as long as possible.

The next few minutes were a blur of activity. Faces were washed, teeth vigorously cleaned, clothes changed and housework rattled through. By the time the welfare woman had got past Sophie, the house was spick-and-span, and a freshly scrubbed Callum and Rose met her at the door.

Rose extended a hand to the bemused woman. "So pleased to meet you. Welcome to my home. Do come in and have a cup of tea," she said with a smile that would have melted ice.

Callum lay on his bed, forced to have an afternoon nap by his gran, who'd spent most of the day fussing over him. The interview with the welfare officer went exceptionally well and, much to everyone's relief and joy, Rose was granted permission to continue her guardianship and to apply to adopt Callum.

After the welfare officer left, Callum explained everything and Rose had driven them (very cautiously) to Shark Bay to pick up Jinx. Sophie and Jinx were then cleaned up and taken back home. The school and Jinx's parents were informed that they had all been struck by a mystery illness and needed the day off to rest. Sophie's parents were unconvinced by her hasty excuse for sneaking out and she was grounded for a week.

They made a pact that the adventures of the night before would remain a secret between the four of them. There was nothing to be gained by telling anyone. The bad bomb had been destroyed, Lester was missing, presumed eaten, goodness had been restored to the people of the city and everyone was safe. Rose also pointed out that the children were technically guilty of breaking and entering, destroying property and hijacking a forklift, and she doubted the authorities would be as forgiving as she was.

The midday news had a report on the mysterious earthquake that destroyed a city warehouse. Seismic experts were confounded. They'd never seen a quake that was localized to just one building before. The report said no one was killed by the quake but the proprietor of Big Al's Used Car Parts had been reported missing and several of his employees were injured. The men suffered from a range of wounds including breaks, bruises, contusions and, most curiously, bee stings. Police had sealed off the area and investigations into the incident were classified.

Callum briefly wondered what had happened to Lester. A part of him believed the hideous man had survived and was on the loose, eager to start rebuilding his evil brain-sucking machines.

Oh, well, the boy thought. If he does resurface, we'll just have to stop him again. With the help of his friends he could do anything. As Callum drifted off to sleep, he was thankful to be safely home, but most of all he was thankful for being able to be thankful.

# ACKNOWLEDGEMENTS

A great number of people assisted in bringing this book to print, so if you don't like it, they're to blame.

Firstly, my reading guinea pigs – Kerrie, Dave, Jackson, Marcus, Lachie and Ella, all enthusiastic *Brain Sucker* fans; also Alix, Struan, East and Hale; plus Matt and Mckenzie Bolland and my lovely niece Maria – your feedback was brilliant. Cheers Jules for the proofread.

Thanks to Luke who helped me work out the mechanics of the slapping spoon. And to author Brian Falkner, who doesn't know me from a bar of soap, but has been extremely generous with his time and support.

Huge thanks to Mike Spindle, the managing director and inventor of the Trekinetic All Terrain wheelchair, which was a major inspiration for the Thunderkit. I love Mike's philosophy of creating a functional, quality product that also looks cool. The Thunderkit is a mix of several designs and the result is purely fictional, especially once Sophie has finished with it.

Now to the publishing professionals. My assessors – Barbara Else and Jill Marshall, your insights really helped me hone my manuscript. Then, of course, my amazingly patient agent – Barbara Mobbs; how you didn't give up on me in the first few months is nothing short of a miracle. Your advice and counsel have been invaluable.

And most importantly thanks to everyone at Walker Books in Australia and in the UK. Everyone has been incredibly enthusiastic and professional. Special mention to Sarah Foster for her support and encouragement (and for deciding to take a risk on me) and to Jess Owen, my editor, who has been, quite simply, awesome. The UK team have been equally fantastic. Thanks to Gill Evans for championing my book, Claire Sandeman for her enthusiasm and general loveliness and Jack Noel for my UK cover design and brain-sucker-like type.

Finally, well done, Glenn; it took a while, but you got there. Apologies to anyone I've forgotten.

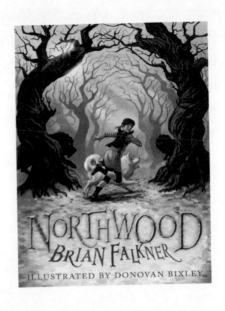

Cecilia Undergarment likes a challenge.
So when she discovers a sad and neglected dog,
she is determined to rescue him.
Unfortunately, her daring attempt lands her lost
and alone in the dark forest of Northwood.
A forest in which ferocious lions roam and those
who enter never return.

But then Northwood has never seen the likes of
Cecilia Undergarment before…

# Granny Samurai,
## the Monkey King and I
### John Chambers

Granny Samurai is small and dangerous to know.
Her teeth are false and so is one of her legs.
Her walking stick conceals a double-action
repeater, of which there are only two in the world.
She has other weapons too, which I am not at
liberty to reveal. What I can reveal is contained
within the pages of this book.

My name is Samuel Johnson. This is our story.

Presenting SAM SWANN – Star of Stage & Screen!
(Well, screen.)
(Well, more of a background role, really…)

My dad, special effects make-up artist to the stars,
lets me go with him when he's working on location.
To be honest, me and Watson (the most loyal and
obedient dog in the universe – as long as I've got food
in my pocket) are pretty happy hanging out behind the
scenes. That's where all the action happens…